Romance Unbound Publishing

Presents

Slave Island

Claire Thompson

Edited by

Donna Fisk

Jae Ashley

Cover Design

Kelly Shorten

Print ISBN 978-1493617593

Dedicated to my dear friend and editor, Donna, whose strength and loving spirit shines through everything she does. Thank you, Donna, for your generous and creative assistance in bringing Julianna's story to life.

Chapter 1

Julianna was sandwiched in between two overweight businessmen with laptops and headphones. At least neither one tried to make small talk. The flight attendant reached over one of the men to hand her a glass of orange juice.

"Is Florida your final destination?"

"Barbados." Julianna smiled. She still could barely believe her luck. After she'd signed the contract, agreeing to allow her image and testimonial to be used in the spa advertising campaign in exchange for the seven day all-expenses-paid vacation, Colin Harris had ironed out the details with her over a cup of coffee at a café around the corner from the salon. She'd still half-expected him to come on to her, but he'd been all business, giving her an itinerary sheet that included her airline ticket confirmation number and details of the flight, along with the name of the limousine service that would be waiting for her at the airport in Barbados.

"Lucky you," the attendant enthused. "I love the Caribbean this time of year—shoot, any time of year!" Julianna was excited. Something good was happening to her at last. She settled back, trying to get comfortable in the narrow seat. Closing her eyes, she began to daydream about white sand, blue water and the week of paradise that awaited her.

~*~

Julianna had just retrieved her bag when she noticed a short dark-skinned man holding up a placard that read: *Paradise Spa – Julianna Beckett*. She waved until she caught his eye. He moved silently toward her.

"Hi," she said. "I'm Julianna Beckett."

The man nodded but said nothing, which Julianna found curious after all the smiling faces and helpful people she'd encountered so far in the airport. It was late, nearly 10:30 at night, and he'd probably rather be home in bed, she reasoned. Though she had planned on getting a soda or bottle of water, she didn't want to keep the driver waiting. Plenty of time to relax with a drink in her sumptuous room at the spa, she thought with a happy sigh. She allowed the man to take her bag and followed him out into the warm, damp air, such a marked change from the freezing winter she'd left behind in New York.

He popped the trunk of a black sedan and placed her suitcase inside. Then he opened the back door of the car and gestured for her to enter. As they drove away from the airport Julianna leaned back against the seat, suddenly aware of how exhausted she was. Soon, she thought, she'd be nestled between soft, clean sheets, the soothing sound of the ocean lulling her to sleep.

About twenty minutes later the driver pulled into a small parking lot that bordered a wooden platform where several speedboats were docked. He beeped the horn three times in quick succession, and leaving the car still running, climbed out. Julianna lowered her window and looked out, confused. She didn't see anything that looked like a resort. In fact, the only nearby structure was an old shack with a crudely painted sign over its door with the words *Charlie's Bait & Beer.*

The man opened her door. She stepped out, a rising sense of unease moving through her. "Excuse me, but I think you've made a mistake. I'm supposed to be taken to the Paradise Spa. Where are we?"

"You take boat," he informed her cryptically.

"What? The spa's on this island. What do you mean I take a boat?" The unease was threatening to bloom into panic, but Julianna forced her voice to remain steady and calm. Surely there was just some misunderstanding.

"You take boat," he repeated gruffly. The door to the shack opened and two men came out of it, both dressed in black shirts and black jeans, one with dark blond hair cut close to his head, the other with stringy black hair falling into his eyes. They looked to be in their twenties, both tall with muscular builds.

They approached Julianna and the driver. "Thanks, Omari." The man spoke with an American accent. He handed an envelope to the driver. "We'll take it from here."

"Excuse me," Julianna interjected. "I'm supposed to have been taken to the Paradise Spa in St. James." She held out her confirmation paper. "This driver has gotten his wires crossed, apparently."

The driver walked back to his car, climbed in and slammed the door. "Hey!" Julianna yelled, "Come back here! This isn't where I'm supposed to be dropped off!" She started toward the driver's side, but the dark-haired man gripped her arm, holding her back.

"Let go of me!" she cried, jerking her arm away. "That guy is supposed to take me to the Paradise Spa. Come back! You have my suitcase, all my things!" She ran after the car, which was already receding down the narrow road into the darkness.

Quickly overtaking her, the man grabbed her by the arm again and yanked her back. This time his grip was too tight and she couldn't pull free. His fingers pressed hard into her muscle. "He has my suitcase," she pleaded. "He's supposed to take me to the spa! Let go of me! You're hurting me!"

"Calm down. You're just going to make it harder on yourself. There's been a change of plans. You're not going to the spa. You're coming with us," the blond guy said.

"Let me go this second! I'm an American citizen. I'll go to the embassy. I'll have you arrested!" She tried to sound authoritative, though her voice was shaking.

"I don't think so." The blond guy grabbed hold of Julianna's purse and pulled it from her arm. She lunged toward him but the dark-haired man wrapped his arms around her from behind, pinning her back against his chest.

Anger, confusion and terror whipped through Julianna as she struggled fruitlessly in her captor's grip.

What in god's name was happening? Was she being kidnapped by the driver and these thugs at random, or had this whole thing been orchestrated well in advance? Her mind flashed on Colin Harris, the handsome older British gentleman who had come into Sophie's Salon where Julianna was a stylist, asking specifically for her. How smooth he'd been when explaining the details of the arrangement.

At the time it had seemed too good to be true, but she'd pushed aside any qualms, too excited over the prospect of a free vacation at a luxury resort. The link he'd given her had seemed legitimate when she'd checked it out online, and she'd even met with another young woman who had claimed she'd done three tours already for the company, and each one had been better than the last. Too good to be true…

"Give me that! Give me my purse!" She jerked hard against the man holding her, looking wildly around the deserted lot. "Help me! Someone, help me!"

"Save your breath. There's no one around for miles. Things will go a lot better for you if you just calm down," the blond guy said. Shoving her purse under his arm, he said to the other man, "Let's go." He took firm hold of one of Julianna's arms so she was trapped between them. They moved toward the dock, dragging her along.

"No!" she cried again. "Let me go!" If they managed to get her onto a boat, she'd be as good as dead, she was sure of it. Desperately she struggled between them and managed to jerk her arms back, elbowing one of the men in the gut. This caused him to release his grip for a second, and she wrenched herself free, kicking out with all her might at the other man's groin.

"Fucking bitch!" The dark-haired man fell to his knees, clutching himself.

The other guy was on her in a flash, grabbing her from behind, pressing a strong arm across her throat. "Get used to the idea you're coming with us. If you would rather be bound and tossed in the bottom of the boat, that can be arranged. If you want to travel upright, you better behave, got it?"

In dazed terror, Julianna nodded as best she could with an arm over her throat. Thankfully, the man relaxed his grip. He looked at the man still on the ground. "You okay, Vince?"

"Yeah." The man called Vince rose to his feet with a groan, still cupping his crotch with one hand. "Stupid cunt." He glared at Julianna. "Let's get her to the island pronto and let the bosses deal with her."

He jumped down into the largest boat moored to the dock. As if she were a sack of potatoes, the blond guy lifted her and passed her over to Vince.

"No, no! You can't do this! No!" Desperately Julianna tried to wrench herself free, leaning over the side of the listing boat. The blond guy set about releasing the moorings from the dock, moving quickly. Vince pinned her right arm behind her back, wrenching it painfully while at the same time reaching around with his other hand to smack her hard in the face.

Julianna cried out in shock and pain. The blond guy turned from what he was doing and looked at them. "Damn it, Vince. You know better than that," he said in a warning tone. "You know Jason doesn't like the goods damaged before he gets a proper look."

The goods. The words at once terrified Julianna while giving her a glimmer of hope. If she was to be presented to someone else, and treated as "the goods", at least they weren't planning on killing her—yet.

"Sorry, Jay. She had it coming, though." Thankfully, he let go of the arm behind her back, but only to yank her down beside him in the back of the boat, catching her in a sort of rough embrace, her back against his chest, his thick fingers digging into her upper arms.

Jay moved to the helm of the speedboat, taking the wheel. He turned the key and the engine roared to life. As the boat moved away from the shore, Julianna felt faint with fear. What were they going to do with her? The boat sped quickly through the water. The wind whipped her hair into her face but the man's grip prevented her from doing anything about it. Her heart was pounding, her mouth dry with fear, her body rigid in his tight hold.

After maybe twenty or thirty interminable minutes she saw lights ahead and could make out the shoreline of a small island. Within a minute they pulled up beside a small dock. Jay cut the engine and eased the boat in beside the platform. He jumped out.

As he was securing the lines Vince hauled Julianna roughly to her feet and jerked her toward the side of the boat. Jay reached for her and pulled her up onto the dock. Vince leered at her, violating her with his eyes. "I can't wait to get my hands on this one. I always did have a thing for redheads."

"Shut it, Vince." Jay snapped. "They're waiting."

"Yeah, whatever." Again on either side of her, the men propelled her toward a small white building. Vince leaned down and spoke in her ear. His breath was sour. "You a *real* redhead, little girl?"

Julianna turned her head away, not responding. He laughed. "Don't matter if you answer. We'll find out soon enough." Julianna shuddered, a tremor of horror and fear that moved through her body and left her shivering, despite the warm night air. When they got to the building's entrance Jay pulled the door open. They pushed Julianna inside, each still grasping an arm.

As they moved down the hall Julianna tried to get her brain to function, but it had turned to mush. All she could think was that she had to get out of there. She had to get away.

They led her to a large room with lots of heavy, dark furniture. The floor was covered by an expensive-looking Oriental rug and oil paintings hung on the walls. They led her to the center of the room, each keeping a firm grip on her arms.

On a long, deep sofa set against one wall sat a man of medium height with a wiry build. His hair was silver, his eyes a steely matching gray. He was holding a brandy snifter, and was dressed in a white short-sleeved shirt and gray slacks. He stared at her, his gaze so intense she felt as if he could see through her. It was very disconcerting and she looked away.

Her eye was drawn by the sound of ice clinking into a glass. Across the room stood a tall man, younger than the other, with a shaved head, a gold hoop earring and a thick black mustache and goatee. He was pouring liquor from a bottle into a cocktail glass, a lit cigar dangling from the corner of his mouth.

He removed the cigar and appraised Julianna with a wolf's smile. "Nice job, boys. Did she give you any trouble?"

Vince started to speak, but Jay cut in, "No more than what you'd expect, Boss. Everything went smooth as clockwork."

"Excellent." The man puffed on his cigar and took a long drink from his glass. Setting the cigar in the edge of a large glass ashtray, he moved from behind the bar and approached them. Up close, his eyes were like cold, dead marbles. A long, thin scar ran from the outer corner of his left eye to his chin. He reeked of whiskey and cigar smoke.

As he bent toward her, Julianna shrank back against her captors but they held her fast. She turned her head away, closing her eyes and bracing herself for she knew not what. He gripped her chin in one large hand, forcing her to face him. Julianna opened her eyes, hiccupping a gasp of terror.

After staring at her a long moment, the man let her go. He turned to the man on the sofa. "What do you think, Stephen? Will we get our money's worth?"

"Without a doubt, Jason." The man on the sofa leaned forward, cradling the snifter in both hands. His voice was surprisingly deep and in another circumstance, Julianna would have found it pleasing. He rose and approached them. The man called Jason stepped back.

Stephen stood only a few inches taller than Julianna but something in his bearing made it seem as if he were looming over her. "Please," she tried, "there's been a horrible mistake. I'm an American citizen."

Stephen lifted his eyebrows, his tone amused. "So am I. But you're not in Kansas anymore, Dorothy. And there truly is no place like home, not for you, not any longer."

"What?" Julianna's voice came out as a squeak.

"You've been abducted, kidnapped, stolen, call it what you like. There is no way off the island, save by boat or helicopter, neither of which you will have access to. That is, not until the proper time."

He stepped back, his steely gaze sweeping over her. "From this moment forward, you have no free will. You are chattel, purchased at a substantial price, but one we hope to double or even triple once you're properly trained. Forget your past. Your best bet going forward is to do as you're told. *Exactly* as you're told, or suffer the consequences."

"You can't…I won't…" Julianna felt faint. She sagged back against the men still holding her. "Please, this can't be happening…"

"It has happened. The sooner you reconcile yourself to your fate, the better off you'll be." He looked down at his watch. "It's late. We'll talk about it in much greater detail in the morning." He turned toward the other man. "Unless you have something else you want to add, Jason?"

"No, they can take her to the hole. A night there should put in her in a more proper frame of mind."

Julianna struggled against the men holding her. "Please! You can't do this." Desperately she tried to think of something that would get her out of this nightmare. "I can pay you, I won't tell—"

Jason waved his hand toward Jay and Vince and turned away as if wearied by her pleas. "Take her away." The men dragged Julianna out of the building, pulling her along as she stumbled between them.

The compound was lit at intervals by tall streetlamps that cast an eerie glow over the area. They moved past several small buildings and bungalows through some palm trees toward a fenced-in enclosure. Opening the gate, they pushed her inside and then let her go with a shove. Julianna stumbled forward, catching herself before she fell. She whirled to face them. "Please. Let me go. I'm begging you."

"Out of our hands, babe." Jay shrugged, looking almost apologetic, while Vince just smirked. "Every new girl spends her first night in the hole."

The hole. It sounded horrible, like something out of a prisoner-of-war camp during the Vietnam War. She would be thrust down into a slimy pit filled with mud, with insects and rats crawling over her. She wrapped her arms around her body and realized she was trembling violently. "No," she whispered. "Please don't do this. You can't." She looked desperately around the enclosure, a last lingering thought of escape still alive inside her. The men were blocking the gate and the fence was too high to climb, even if she could somehow get past them.

"Sorry, kid, boss's orders." Jay said. "It's not so bad. You'll be fine." Putting his arm forcibly around Julianna's shoulders, he propelled her toward a metal grate set into the ground. She watched helplessly as he took a chain from around his neck and used a key at the end of it to open a padlock secured to a thick iron ring that held the grate closed. Once he'd released the lock, he pulled the grate open.

"No," Julianna whispered, too stunned to speak louder. This couldn't be happening. It wasn't real. Things like this didn't happen in real life. Not to hairstylists from Manhattan.

Vince approached Julianna and put his hands over her breasts, cupping them as she shrank back. He looked past her to Jay. "What do you think, Jay? Do we strip her now? I'm still damn curious to know if she's a natural redhead."

"No." Jay replied. "You know the policy on that. If they find out you were taking first dibs—"

"How would they know? This piece of ass ain't gonna squeal on me, are ya', bitch?" He squeezed her breasts through her blouse.

"I said no." Jay's voice was firm. "Get your hands off her and help me get her in the hole."

"All right, all right," Vince said, dropping his hands. "I was just foolin' around anyway."

They moved on either side of her and lifted Julianna from the ground. "No, no, no!" she cried, struggling as they lowered her into the small confines of the hole. She kicked out wildly as they held her aloft over the hole, terrified of being left in there. "Let me go! Let me go, let me go!" she screamed, twisting violently in their strong grip.

They dropped her down into the hole. As they lowered the iron grate, she was forced to crouch down in a kneeling position. The space wasn't deep enough for her to stand, nor wide enough for her to lie down. The grate came down over her head with a clang and she could hear the sound of the padlock being clicked into place. She tried to lift herself enough to see the men through the grate, but all she could see was the sky, black and studded with tiny stars.

Reaching up, she gripped the bars and pushed with all her might, but they didn't budge. She felt the walls of the enclosure. They were rough and cool to the touch, and appeared to be concrete. Beneath her feet was sandy dirt but it was dry and, mercifully, seemed to be insect- and vermin-free. Julianna slumped to the ground, dropping her head into her hands.

Her jeans and panties were damp and she realized with dismay that in the tumult of them thrusting her into the pit she'd wet herself. "Someone, help me," she whimpered. Surely they wouldn't really leave her here all night? "Hello?" she called out, timidly at first, and then with more volume, but she heard nothing, save the sound of the ocean.

Tears streaked down her cheeks and her whimpers erupted into all-out crying. She hid her face in her hands, her body wracked with sobbing. She cried until there were no tears left and still no one came for her. Rubbing her tear and snot-smeared face with the bottom of her blouse, wearily Julianna leaned back against the wall of the small enclosure and looked upward at the dark night sky.

Though she'd never considered herself a religious person, Julianna lowered her head, clasped her hands beneath her chin and began to pray.

Chapter 2

Julianna's eyes sprang open when she heard the sound of the gate being opened and the murmur of voices. The sun was shining overhead. Somehow, despite her discomfort and misery, she'd managed to doze for a while. She was curled on her side in the dirt, the arm beneath her head completely asleep. She struggled upright, every muscle in her body protesting.

Pushing her tangled hair from her face, she peered upward, straining to hear what was going on above her. She heard the footsteps moving closer, and then the click of the padlock as it was opened. A moment later the iron-barred grate was lifted and strong arms reached down, catching Julianna beneath her arms and hauling her up and out of the hole.

"Holy shit, you look like something the cat dragged in." Vince eyed her as she slumped to the ground. He turned to Jay, rubbing his hands together. "Let's hose her down. You don't want sand in your girlfriend's bungalow."

Jay scowled at Vince, but said nothing. Julianna felt dizzy and weak, her mouth dry as bone. "Thirsty." The word came out in a croak.

"What's that?" Jay crouched down beside her, leaning in close. Today the two men were dressed in white—white shorts and T-shirts with flip-flops on their feet.

"Thirsty," she repeated.

"Get the hose, Vince," Jay said, gesturing with his chin. Turning back to Julianna he said, "You can have some water from the hose. Then Alma will get you ready."

Vince approached holding a long green garden hose with a nozzle on the end. He turned the nozzle and water began to pour from the hose, creating a dark pattern against the sandy dirt. She watched it, her thirst like a flame. Vince held it near her mouth. Julianna knelt up on her haunches and leaned forward, slurping at the cold, delicious water as best she could.

The worst of her thirst had abated, though she would have liked more, when Vince twisted the nozzle, shutting off the stream. He jerked the hose away. "Get up and get out of those filthy clothes," he ordered. "You stink."

Julianna stared from one man to the other, the entreaties rising to her lips finding no voice. Miserably, she hauled herself to her feet and reached for the top button of her blouse. Her fingers were trembling and she found it hard to get the button open.

"Hurry it up, or we'll do it for you," Vince barked. Julianna glanced to her left and right, wondering if there was anyone else on this island—anyone who could help her. She saw no one. "We don't got all day." Vince reached for her blouse with both hands and ripped it open, sending the buttons flying. Julianna gasped and tried to clutch the blouse closed. Ignoring her, Vince reached for her jeans, jerking the snap and tugging the zipper as he dragged them down her legs.

"What'd ya' do, piss yourself?" he said, wrinkling his nose as he pulled at the denim. "Doesn't matter—you won't be needing these clothes again." Jay knelt beside her, pulling off Julianna's sneakers and socks so Vince could pull the jeans away.

Julianna was left in only her bra and panties, trying vainly to cover her body with her hands. "Better not do that in front of the bosses," Vince said in a warning voice. He took a small penknife from his shorts pocket and flicked it open. Before Julianna could react, he hooked the tip of it beneath her bra between her breasts and sliced through the fabric. When he pointed the knife at her panties, Julianna stepped back, pulling them off herself with shaking hands.

Vince whistled, ogling her. "Natural redhead, yeah baby."

"Keep your dick in your pants, dude," Jay said, though he, too, was staring at her body while Julianna blushed hotly. "We've got a job to do. You don't want to keep them waiting."

"Yeah, yeah, whatever," Vince replied. He aimed the hose at Julianna and twisted the nozzle until a high-pressured spray shot from it. "Arms over your head." In a daze of fear Julianna obeyed, closing her eyes as the cold water blasted over her body. Vince moved around her as if she was an animal or a tree stump, soaking her with the needling spray. Unable to help herself she dropped her arms, wrapping them around herself as she shivered.

"Good enough," Jay said, glancing at his watch. "Let's get her over to Alma."

They marched the naked, shivering girl out of the gate and through the palm trees toward a wooden bungalow. The door opened as they approached and a young woman with dark skin and almond shaped eyes stood just inside. Her hair was pulled back in a thick ponytail and she was wearing a white sleeveless dress, sheer enough to show her dark nipples beneath it. She crooked a finger toward Julianna, gesturing for her to enter.

"We'll wait out here," Jay said, pulling a pack of cigarettes from his pocket and tapping one into his hand. As he was handing the pack to Vince, the woman closed the door.

She handed a large towel to Julianna, which she took gratefully and wrapped around her body. The woman, probably in her early twenties, looked kind and for the first time since the night before, Julianna felt a glimmer of hope. "Please," she ventured. "Where are we? You've got to help me get out of here!"

The woman shook her head. "Shh," she said very softly, her lips barely moving. "They can hear you." She gestured with her head toward a black globe set into the ceiling. Julianna realized it was a camera and that it probably contained a microphone as well.

In a louder voice, the woman said, "My name is Alma. I will prepare you for presentation." She spoke with an accent, a pleasing lilt in her voice. Julianna understood she wouldn't or couldn't answer Julianna's question, and the hope that had risen a moment before was quickly doused.

Alma led Julianna to a curtained-off area in the corner of the room. She opened the curtain, revealing a small shower stall. There was soap and bottles of shampoo and conditioner. Alma reached into the stall and turned on the water and pulled the curtain closed. "Shower quickly and wash your hair."

Not knowing what else to do, Julianna stepped into the shower, enjoying the hot, soothing spray in spite of the situation. She stood with her head back, letting the water cascade over her. "Hurry," Alma whispered on the other side of the curtain. Julianna reached for the shampoo and lathered her hair. As she was soaping her body, the water suddenly went from hot to tepid and rapidly to cold. Julianna shut off the water.

She peeked past the curtain. Alma was standing there with the towel. Julianna rubbed her hair with it and then wrapped it around her body. She stared at Alma, wondering if this woman was there of her own free will.

Alma took a second towel and laid it on the floor. She pointed. "Lie down and spread your legs. I will shave you."

"What?" Julianna didn't move.

"It's essential that you be smooth for your presentation. The girls are always kept smooth here on the island. You will be shaved daily. Be glad it's me this first time and not one of the guards. They aren't always so careful with the razor."

The girls. So there were other women here, women like her. How many? Where were they kept? What were they kept for? She shuddered, her mind refusing to dwell on the horrible possibilities.

Alma went behind a screened partition and Julianna could hear the sound of water running. A moment later she returned with a bowl of soapy water, a can of shaving cream and a razor. Could that razor be used as a weapon, Julianna wondered. Even if she did get hold of it, how much damage could a safety razor inflict? She didn't want to hurt Alma; she only wanted to escape.

Alma pointed again to the floor and then glanced at the camera. "Please," she said softly. "You will pay a heavy price if you disobey. Don't let that happen, I beg you."

Frightened by these words, Julianna knelt on the towel and lay back, letting her own towel fall open. Alma shaved her underarms and legs first, before focusing on her pubic hair, which was sparse to begin with. She was careful, moving in slow even strokes over Julianna's pubic mound and labia, running a light finger in the wake of the razor. Julianna kept her eyes closed, holding herself as still as possible as the sharp blades scraped gently over her skin. She had never been so embarrassed in her life.

Finally satisfied, Alma sat back. "There," she said. "That's done. Now for your hair and makeup." She allowed Julianna to wrap the towel around herself again, and led her to a small vanity with a mirror over it, a low stool set in front of it. The single-room bungalow was actually a rather pleasant space, the neatly made bed and vanity adding a feminine touch. The bare walls were whitewashed and windows set into opposite sides of the room let the sun stream in through pale blue, gauzy curtains. Against one wall stood a clothing rack filled with white dresses of varying lengths and sizes.

"Sit on the stool, please." Julianna sat down, facing the mirror. There was a bruise on her face where the man had struck her on the boat and her eyes were puffy and red from crying the night before. She touched the bruise and looked at Alma in the mirror, blurting in terror, "What's going to happen to me?" A sharp look from the woman made her lower her voice to a whisper. "What is this place? Where are we? Please, you have to tell me."

Alma shook her head. "Hush. No questions. Not now. They always listen on the first day especially." She cast a nervous glance back at the camera and shook her head again. In a louder voice, she said, "We need to choose a dress for you." She eyed Julianna in the mirror, pursing her lips and tilting her head. She went to the clothes rack and returned holding a dress. "Try this on."

Julianna sighed in defeat, certain now Alma would tell her nothing. She stood, pulling the dress over her head and letting the towel fall. The silky garment hung loosely to just above the knee. Though it was sheer, and no underwear was being offered, it was definitely better than nothing.

"What size shoe do you wear?" Alma asked.

"Seven and a half."

Alma went to the dress rack and Julianna now noticed a row of shoe boxes set beneath it. Alma selected and brought it to her. The shoes inside were black and shiny with very high heels—nothing Julianna would ever choose for herself. For the moment, Alma set them aside.

Alma gestured for her to sit again and Julianna obeyed. She dried Julianna's hair with a blow dryer and fluffed it with her fingers. "You have lovely hair," she said, "and such fair skin." She shook her head as if this observation was cause for pity rather than praise.

Jay opened the door and leaned in. "We about done here?" He flashed a smiled at Alma and she smiled back, a real smile, though a very brief one. As she turned away, her face smoothed back into a neutral expression. "Yes, very nearly done." He nodded and shut the door.

"We must hurry," Alma said. "I think I can conceal that mark." Lightly she touched the bruise left by Vince's hand. Pulling a plastic box from beneath the counter, she reached in and took out a bottle of foundation and container of cotton balls. Julianna closed her eyes as the woman applied makeup to her cheeks, eyes and lips. The experience was surreal—being prepared as if she were an object for display and sale.

"I'm so afraid," she said, tears forming in her eyes.

"I know. I'm sorry. Don't cry. You'll mess up the mascara." As she applied the makeup to Julianna's face, Alma leaned close, her mouth just beside Julianna's ear, her voice barely a whisper. "Focus on what you can control. They can imprison your body but don't let them break your spirit." In a louder voice, she said, "See how lovely you look." Julianna followed Alma's gaze and saw herself in the mirror, her hair falling in shiny waves to her shoulders, the makeup expertly applied, wide eyes staring back at her with a look of stark fear.

The door swung open again and Vince entered the bungalow. "Let's go," he barked. "Time's up. She better be ready, Alma, or—" He stopped mid-threat and stared at Julianna, raising his thick eyebrows. "Nice," he said, drawing out the word with evident appreciation. "She cleans up pretty good. Jesus, if I had the money, *I'd* buy her."

Julianna felt Alma's cool fingers on her arm. "Courage," Alma whispered.

Jay stepped inside and the two men moved toward her. Instinctively Julianna took a step back, but there was nowhere to go. She was given a pair of flip-flops to wear as she was led away between the two men. Jay held the shoebox beneath one arm. As they walked along a path they passed a long single-story building made out of the same white brick as the building she'd been to the night before. It had the feel of an army barracks, or worse, a prison. There were a few windows but they were set high along the walls and covered with bars. There was no one in sight.

As they walked in the daylight she saw the perimeter of the island was ringed by palms trees, past which she guessed lay the sandy shores and the dock.

She realized as she walked that not only was she still thirsty, she was starving. "Can I get something to eat?" she asked as they hustled her along.

"That's up to the bosses," Jay said. "They'll take care of all that." This was a less than satisfying answer, but Julianna had learned enough already to know that was the end of the discussion.

Once inside the building they stopped in front of the same room as the night before. This time the door was closed. Jay opened the shoebox and removed the shoes, placing them on the floor in front of Julianna. "Put them on," he said.

"I don't think I can walk in those," Julianna protested.

"You better learn how fast," Vince snapped.

With a sigh, Julianna slipped off the flip-flops and stepped into the high heels that forced her feet into Barbie-doll arches. Jay knocked on the door and it was pulled open by Stephen, who stepped back, gesturing for them to enter.

Jay and Vince led her to a corner of the room that had been set up like a photo studio, with a black sheet draped against the wall, and bright camera lights placed in front of it. A stool sat to one side. There was a large camera on a tripod and Jason stood near it, watching as Julianna was led to stand in front of the camera. The two men let her go and stepped away. Julianna stood uncertainly, trying to stay balanced on the high heels as she wrapped her arms around herself.

Jason assumed his position behind the camera. "We're going to get some pictures for your portfolio. Just stand naturally, hands at your sides." He began to take pictures. "Don't look so frightened," he ordered, still clicking. "Smile."

Julianna tried to force her lips into something that approximated a smile. This whole thing was so surreal she was having a hard time grasping it. "Hands on your hips. Turn to the left. Drop your chin a little. Yes...good." He continued to click for a while and then unscrewed the camera from its tripod and moved closer.

"Lift your dress up to your waist." It was Stephen who spoke, his voice calmly matter-of-fact. Julianna stared from him to Jason and back again without moving to obey.

Stephen glowered at her, taking a step toward her. It was her against four men. She knew she either did what they said now, or after they forced her. Frightened and embarrassed, Julianna touched the hem of the flimsy dress. Swallowing hard, she lifted the edges, revealing her shaven mons for the camera.

"Sit on the stool," Jason said. "Lift the dress first. Bare ass on the stool." Biting her lip, Julianna obeyed. "Spread your legs, show the camera that pretty little cunt." Her face flaming, Julianna scooted to the edge of the stool, dying a thousand deaths as he knelt before her, the camera nearly touching her as he snapped shot after shot.

She was ordered to bend over the stool, exposing her bare ass to the camera and again forced to spread her legs in that position. They made her cup her breasts and finger herself, all the while clicking away. Finally Stephen said, "I think we have enough, Jason. Do you agree?"

"Yeah, okay. We'll do the bondage shots later, once she's got a little training under her belt." He smacked his lips and ran the tip of his tongue over them while he raked Julianna with an insolent, hungry stare. *Bondage shots.* Julianna felt ice trickling through her veins.

Stephen moved closer to her, scanning a clipboard he held in his hand. "You're twenty-three, originally from Mahwah, New Jersey. Your mother is dead, father unknown. You currently reside in Queens, New York, and work as a hairstylist in Manhattan at an establishment called Sophie's Salon. You have no criminal record. You stand five-foot, four inches tall and weigh 110 pounds. You've never had a broken bone and you have all your teeth. Your vision is twenty-twenty and you've been sexually active since the age of eighteen. No STDs."

Julianna, eyes wide with shock, whispered, "How do you know all that?"

"We do our homework. Or rather, our operatives in the field do. I'm telling you all this because I want you to understand this wasn't a random abduction. You were carefully selected, once you were initially identified as someone with potential."

"Colin Harris," Julianna murmured. The whole thing had been one big sham—the business card, the receptionist answering at the other end, who just *happened* to know someone local who was eager to meet and clinch the deal with her lies. *Too good to be true…*

"Is that what he called himself this time?" Jason interjected, grinning beneath the drooping mustache.

Julianna felt lightheaded. Her ears were ringing and a gripping nausea moved through her empty stomach. Stephen approached her and took her arm, leading her to a sofa, where she collapsed against the deep cushions. "This is a nightmare," she moaned. "This can't be happening. Why are you doing this? Please, please let me go. I want to go home." Dropping her head into her hands, Julianna burst into tears.

Stephen sat on a chair catty-corner to the sofa and put his hand on Julianna's knee. "Julianna," he said, his voice soft but steely. "Stop crying and look at me. Now." Julianna looked up slowly from her hands, sniffling. "I'm going to tell you just exactly how things stand. The sooner you accept the situation, the better it will be for you. The fact is, you are never going back. You have basically ceased to exist. At least, Julianna Beckett has ceased to exist.

"From this moment forward you are nothing more than property. Any man on this island has full rights to your body, as long as they don't harm or impregnate you. Resisting anyone is grounds for severe punishment, do I make myself clear?"

Julianna stared at Stephen, her mouth hanging open. She felt as if all the breath had been smashed out of her lungs. He continued calmly. "As of this point, until you are placed with a Master, you have no name. While you are here on the island, you have been assigned a number. You are number thirty-eight, and like the thirty-seven who have come before you, you will learn what it is to obey. You will be broken down—all trace of ego and self-will will be summarily and ruthlessly excised from your makeup. You will learn submission in its every dimension.

"We will teach you to become sexualized. The goal is to intertwine torture and sexual pleasure so thoroughly in your psyche that you'll climax as easily from the cane as the cock. You will be trained to serve a man on every possible level. Once you are deemed worthy, you will be sold. If we've done our job properly, you will no longer regard this as a fate worse than death, but as an honor and a privilege to serve and submit."

Julianna stared at the man in speechless horror, too stunned to continue crying. It was impossible to believe what she was hearing. Sanctioned rape, torture, sexual slavery. Submission, punishment, breaking her down in mind and body. He was outlining a living hell more terrifying than anything she could have imagined, speaking in that deep, calm voice as if this were all perfectly normal. Helplessly, Julianna looked from him to Jason, who simply nodded.

Stephen leaned close to her, his chilly gray eyes boring into hers. "Who are you?"

Julianna didn't answer. Stephen stood and, before Julianna could react, slapped her hard across the face and then jerked her by her hair from the couch to her knees. Tears blinded her eyes and her hands moved automatically to touch the spot where he'd struck her.

Julianna looked up, her hand still cradling her cheek. Stephen looked down at her, a grim smile on his face, his eyes hard. "You will always answer a direct question. You are number thirty-eight. I'm going to give you some time to think about your response. When I ask you again, make sure you answer properly."

He turned to Vince and Jay. "Take number thirty-eight to solitary confinement."

Chapter 3

Julianna lay on a narrow army cot. She was in a one-room hut with a low ceiling and no windows. The walls were made from bamboo poles lashed together with rope. The crude door was locked from the outside by means of a wooden two-by-four wedged into place across it. The ceiling was made of tin, held up with rough wooden beams. In a corner where the wall met the roof she saw the black dome, like a lidless eye gazing at her. What light there was came through the chinks between the bamboo poles. Aside from the cot, the only other thing in the small enclosure were two large plastic buckets, one with water in it that appeared reasonably fresh, the other she assumed was for waste. The air was hot and close, and the smell of feces, sweat and fear saturated the place.

Jay and Vince had taken her from the building and loaded her onto an all terrain vehicle, wedged between the two of them. She'd been driven to the far side of the island where the lone hut stood, set against the backdrop of a sapphire sea.

After shoving her inside, they left without a word. She sat still on the cot for a long time, staring at nothing as hot tears rolled steadily down her cheeks. Eventually she made herself stop. Crying wasn't going to get her out of there. She had to come up with a plan.

Moving to the bucket, she washed her face, using the hem of her dress to dry her skin, and leaving a smear of makeup on the material. Cupping her hands, she brought some water to her lips and drank. It was warm and had a faintly salty taste, but seemed fresh enough. If only she had something to eat to go with it! Her stomach was a tight ball, having moved past hunger into a dull ache.

"I have to get out of here," she whispered. She began to pace restlessly around the small, hot space, peering through various chinks in the bamboo to see what she could see outside. With a surreptitious glance at the camera overhead, she slipped her fingers beneath one of the stout ropes that secured the poles, wondering if somehow she could find a way to undo it. The rope was knotted tightly, its texture rough against her fingers. Using her body to shield what she was doing, she tried to loosen a knot, but met with no success.

Exhausted, she lay down. The cot, while less than satisfactory, was better than the dirt hole she'd spent the previous night in. She closed her eyes and actually managed to fall into an uneasy doze.

She came wide awake at the sound of heavy footsteps clomping up the path. Her heart gave a jump and then settled to a fast, hard beat. She sat bolt upright and swung her legs over the cot, her eyes sweeping the small space as she wished there was somewhere to hide. She heard the sound of the wooden latch being lifted and sucked in a sharp breath of fear. She was sweating, her heart thumping in her ears.

She stood, tense, wiping her sweating palms on her dress as the door swung outward. Stephen stepped inside, a bowl in his hand. She stayed in the corner, wondering if he was alone, wondering if she could somehow overpower him. As a woman living alone in the city, she knew how to defend herself. She had taken several courses in self-defense over the past couple of years since she'd first started working in Manhattan.

Who was she kidding? She hadn't eaten in nearly twenty-four hours and she'd barely slept. Still, if she could take him unaware…

Any hope evaporated as she saw two men dressed in black cargo pants and tank tops, heavy boots on their feet, standing at the entrance. They held large, scary looking whips with lots of thick leather strips, as well as handcuffs and lengths of chain.

As if they weren't even there, Stephen asked, "Are you hungry?" He held out the bowl, which contained what looked like rice and black beans with bits of sausage. The dull ache in her belly transformed into sharp hunger pangs at the sight of the food.

"Yes," she whispered.

"Who are you?"

Julianna stiffened and thrust out her chin. "My name is Julianna. Julianna Beckett."

Stephen shook his head. "Stupid girl. You are number thirty-eight." He stepped into the room. Julianna shrank against the back wall. He held out the bowl of food. Julianna reached for it and he pulled it away. "What is your number?"

Julianna desperately wanted that bowl of food. It smelled heavenly. Her mouth began to water and she had to swallow to keep from choking on her own saliva. "My number..." she began, but she couldn't say it. She wouldn't say it. Goddamn it, she wasn't a fucking number! "My name is Julianna Beckett," she said doggedly.

Stephen shook his head and frowned. He turned toward the men still standing just outside the door. "Beat her."

He pushed his way between the guards, taking the food with him. Julianna cursed herself—why hadn't she been able to say it? Just to get the food? "Wait! I'm number thirty-eight!" she shouted, but Stephen disappeared from view.

The two men moved into the hut. She forgot about the food and the philosophical debate over names and numbers when they advanced upon her. Neither said a word as they grabbed her arms and wrenched them over her head, securing a pair of steel cuffs around her wrists in the process, which they attached to a chain they looped through one of the ropes that formed part of the bamboo walls.

In the space of a few seconds Julianna was bound at the wrists, her body pressed against the wall, her back to the men. One of them grabbed and ripped the dress from her back, easily tearing the flimsy fabric.

"No, please! Please don't hurt me. Please! Oh god, don't hurt me!" Julianna begged, her voice rising in a yelp of fear. They ignored her, their faces impassive when she twisted back toward them to beg.

The leather landed hard on her back, ass and thighs in vicious, stinging blows. Julianna screamed and jerked in her restraints, but the men were relentless, whipping her steadily and thoroughly until Julianna finally sagged in her chains, crying as much from fear as pain as they continued to cover her skin from calf to shoulder with the stinging leather.

As abruptly as they'd started, they stopped. One of the men reached for the cuffs, which he unlocked with a small key and pulled from her now-chafed and aching wrists. She slumped to the floor, curling in a ball and hiding her head, afraid they would start again if she moved.

Mercifully, they turned and left. After a moment she heard the sound of the wooden latch falling into place. She stayed where she was for a long while, rocking back and forth on the rough planks that made up the floor of the hut. Eventually she stood, moving stiffly toward the cot. The skin on her back and ass felt flayed and tender. She lay down carefully on her stomach and cradled her head in her arms.

It was so hot now that she could actually feel the heat radiating down from the tin roof. Sweat rolled from her body, soaking the canvas cot. She drifted in and out of consciousness, her mind blank, save for the terror that knocked and clamored at its edges. After a while she dragged herself from the cot and drank from the water bucket. She splashed a little over her face, afraid to use too much.

Time inched forward as she lay again on the cot, pinned down by the heat, exhaustion and fear. Hours passed, days passed, years passed—at least so it seemed. She was alone. She would be left there to starve, never found, barely missed. She drifted in and out of restless sleep, waking each time with a jolt from murky, terrifying nightmares that were no worse than the nightmare of this reality in which she found herself.

The hut began to darken as the sun went down. The air cooled quickly and Julianna found herself shivering as the sweat evaporated on her body. She began to whisper the same words over and over as she hugged herself and rocked in a vain effort to soothe herself.

"Mama. Where are you, Mama? Come get me please. I want to go home."

~*~

Julianna awoke suddenly to the sound of the ATV approaching. She could hear footsteps coming closer and she tensed, drawing herself into a tight ball on the cot as if that would somehow protect her. She heard the latch being lifted from the door and it was pulled open. It was daylight, and she squinted against the bright sun that entered the hut through the open door, along with Stephen and his henchman.

She saw Stephen was carrying a glass bowl again, this time filled with fresh cut pineapple, bananas, plump green grapes and glistening bits of orange mango. The fragrant aroma of the fruit nearly knocked her over and she gasped as she stared at the bowl, swallowing to keep from choking.

"Please," she whispered.

Stephen set the bowl on the floor in the center of the hut. "Get on the floor," he said brusquely. "Kneel with your head on the ground, ass in the air." He waited a beat and then barked, "Move!"

Julianna rolled from the cot and crouched on the hard floor, glad at least the position allowed her to hide most of her naked body. She touched her forehead to the rough wood, aware she was shaking but unable to stop.

Stephen moved right in front of her, the toe of one huarache sandal pressing under her bowed head. She didn't move. She wanted that fruit. Oh god, she wanted that fruit.

"Who are you?" he asked.

She swallowed. What did it matter? They were only words. A means to an end. "Number thirty-eight," she mumbled into the floor.

"Speak up. I can't hear you." The sandal wedged harder beneath her forehead.

"Number thirty-eight," she said louder, at once hating and forgiving herself.

Stephen chuckled softly above her. "That's right. That's who you are." The foot moved back. "Would you like some fruit, number thirty-eight?"

"Yes, please," she whispered, nearly faint with longing. The banana and pineapple smelled heavenly.

She could almost taste the sweet tang of mango on her tongue.

"Stand up."

Julianna struggled to her feet. She moved too fast, and the dizziness that assailed her made her list and nearly fall, but she managed to right herself. Her eyes slid to the bowl on the floor.

Stephen continued. "When you are given permission to stand, you will assume an at-attention position, legs shoulder-width apart, back straight, fingers locked behind your head, understood?"

Julianna hesitated, her eyes moving over the two men behind Stephen, her gaze catching on the long, thin sticks they held in their hands. Slowly she lifted her arms, locking her fingers behind her head as instructed, keenly aware of her nakedness in front of the three men.

Stephen approached her and reached out. Julianna flinched and shrank back. "At attention!" he shouted. "Never pull away from a trainer, *ever*. No matter what they do to you, you stand there and *take* it. Now, a brief lesson in protocol. You don't speak unless spoken to. You always answer a direct question, and you address every man on this island as sir, do you understand?"

"Yes…sir." Julianna couldn't seem to get her breath, each one shallower than the last. Hunger overrode her fear. "Please, sir" she begged. "I'm so hungry."

Stephen extended his hand again and Julianna closed her eyes, but somehow managed not to flinch away. She was expecting a slap in the face like before, but instead he stroked her cheek, his voice suddenly gentle. "I know you are, thirty-eight. You were a bad girl, and bad girls get punished. But they also get forgiven." His touch was soft, lingering.

A tear rolled down Julianna's cheek. Stephen flicked it away with his thumb. "You would like some of that nice, fresh fruit, wouldn't you, number thirty-eight?" He continued to stroke her cheek.

"Yes. Yes, please...sir."

He stepped back, smiling. "Then you shall have it."

Gratefully, Julianna started to reach for the bowl, but Stephen stopped her.

"Back in position." His voice had resumed its harsh tone. "Hands behind your head."

"But—"

"Never speak unless spoken to."

Julianna bit her lower lip, terrified he was now going to refuse her the fruit. What horrible game was he playing, and how could she learn the rules? She resumed the position, trying not to sway, her head swimming.

"Kneel." Stephen pointed to the ground. "But keep your hands behind your head."

Somehow Julianna managed to lower herself to the floor without falling or losing her position. The bowl was less than a foot away from her. She could see it in her peripheral vision, but she didn't dare turn her head. She stared straight ahead, waiting in quiet desperation.

Stephen crouched in front of her and reached for the fruit. "Open your mouth."

Eagerly as a baby bird, Julianna did as she was told. Stephen picked up a grape and dropped it on her tongue, like some sort of unholy Communion. Julianna bit down, the grape juice bursting inside her mouth like liquid heaven. She had never in her life tasted anything so sweet, so perfect.

He gave her another, and then a piece of pineapple. She tried not to gobble the fruit, but she couldn't help it. Not only was she starving, but she was afraid he might stop at any moment. She wanted all the fruit in that bowl—every bit of it.

When she'd eaten about half of the contents, Stephen set the bowl down on the floor between them. She was still ravenous. The first few bites had awakened her appetite with a vengeance. She managed to swallow the moan of frustration that rose in her throat, certain this would somehow be used against her. She choked back a sigh and focused on the middle distance, longing for withheld the fruit.

"You want more." It was a statement.

"Yes, please," she managed.

"Yes please, *sir*," he amended.

"Yes, sir," she whispered.

He nodded. "As to the fruit, the first few bites were free. But now you have to pay for it." He yanked at her arm, hauling her roughly to her feet.

A surge of terror shot through Julianna's veins. Stephen continued, "For each additional piece of fruit, you will receive one stroke of the cane. Assume an attention position, hands behind your head."

Julianna's eyes darted with fear toward the sticks the guards held in their hands. Canes! Both men were watching her, strong arms crossed over their chests, their faces impassive. One of them had a length of sturdy chain slung over his shoulder.

"I'm—I'm not hungry...sir."

"Don't lie. Not that it matters. You'll do as you're told. You're going to eat the fruit, and you're going to take the cane. Pleasure or pain—it makes no difference. You serve at the pleasure of your Master, no matter what form that pleasure for him takes." He caressed her right breast as he said this, rolling the nipple between his thumb and forefinger.

With a cry, Julianna jerked back from his touch.

"That just cost you five extra strokes, thirty-eight. Do it again and it's another ten."

Julianna squeezed her eyes shut as he handled her other nipple, pulling and twisting it erect. "Open your eyes," he ordered. She did, but suddenly found herself unable to contain the rage behind the fear. If looks could kill, he would have dropped to the ground, his heart stopping before he hit.

He slapped her face twice, once on each cheek. She waited for the barrage of fury sure to follow, but to her surprise he smiled, though his eyes were cruel. "A redheaded spitfire. You can tremble and cry all you like. Don't think I don't see the fire. You might suppose I want to douse it, but I don't."

He shook his head, stroking her hot, stinging cheek with the back of two fingers. "No, we'll keep the flame burning, but simply redirect it, channeling it into the constant lust that befits a sex slave." His hand moved down her torso and he cupped her pussy. Julianna gasped but held her ground, too afraid of his earlier threat to pull away.

He pushed a hard finger into her dry opening and she drew in a sharp breath, hating him. He leaned close, his stale breath hitting her as he wiggled his disgusting finger inside her. She forced herself to stay still, pressing her lips together to keep from screaming.

Finally letting his hand drop, Stephen stepped back and turned toward the men still standing in the doorway.

"Gentlemen, the canes."

The men entered the small hut. As they approached, Julianna's every instinct told her to run, but there was nowhere to go. One of the men grabbed her wrists and held them together while he wrapped a single, thick cuff with a D ring on the outside of it around them, pulling it tight with a Velcro strap. He pulled the chain from his shoulder and threaded it over one of the wooden beams in the low ceiling. He attached one end of a clip to the D ring on the cuff and the other to the chain hanging from the ceiling, which had the effect of forcing Julianna up on tiptoe.

When she started to close her legs to adjust to the tension and lower her feet, Stephen kicked at her ankles. "Legs apart!" Julianna was literally panting with fear.

The dizziness that assailed her once again wasn't only the result of hunger.

"Open your mouth." Stephen pushed his fingers between her lips, dropping a slice of banana on her tongue. Despite her predicament, Julianna savored the fruit, chewing it as slowly as she could.

The guards were standing behind her, out of her line of vision. She saw Stephen nod and then the cane cut through the air and made contact with her ass with a whistling thwack. The pain was far more intense than the flogging the day before. As the seconds passed, it hurt more, not less, a line of burning fire that hurtled through her nerve endings to her brain and erupted from her mouth as a scream. Instinctively, she slammed her legs together. Just as quickly, Stephen kicked them apart.

Stephen held a piece of mango close to her lips. She opened her mouth, the flavor exploding on her tongue as the cane landed on her ass, its stroke just as hard as the first.

Food and then the cane, pleasure and then the pain, over and over, punctuated by her cries, muffled in the seconds when the fruit was dispensed.

"Time for the extra five." She barely heard the words, but she felt the strike of fire, slicing over her ass and thighs and heard the sound of her own screams. She began to pant, unable to fill her lungs, a gray film obscuring her vision...

Julianna opened her eyes, for a moment completely disoriented. She felt the weight at her shackled wrists and realized it was her own body, sagging heavily against them. Her face was damp and felt flushed, and rivulets of sweat rolled down her sides and between her breasts. Her ass and thighs were stinging and burning and she groaned in pain.

"You fainted." Stephen was still standing in front of her, the now-empty bowl of fruit cradled against his chest. "We'll build up your tolerance, once you're in the slave quarters."

He spoke so matter-of-factly, sending a chill down Julianna's spine. He nodded toward the men, who proceeded to unhook her from the chain and remove the cuff from her wrists. She sank to her knees, clutching at her stomach, which was cramping painfully from the fruit after no food for two days.

"Thank me and the boys for your training. That's another rule to get into that pretty head of yours. Whatever is done to you, whether you're in training, or a guard is just using you for his pleasure, you will thank them by kneeling and kissing their foot and saying the words, 'Thank you, sir, for using this worthless slave.'"

Julianna stared at Stephen. She would rather eat dirt than kiss that bastard's foot. As to thanking his thugs for beating her—fuck that! He was watching her face, his eyes narrowing and his expression darkening.

Just do it, an urgent voice whispered in her head. *You took the caning. Do what he says and maybe they'll leave.* Her gut was roiling now. She needed to relieve herself and she was damned if she'd do it in front of these dreadful men.

She bent forward, touching her lips to Stephen's dusty sandal. "Thank you, sir..." The words stuck in her throat but she forced them out. "... for using this slave."

"This worthless slave," he corrected.

"This worthless slave," she repeated through clenched teeth.

Turning, she repeated the process with the two men, brushing her lips over their heavy black boots. Slowly she knelt back up. Stephen was watching her. "Your position. Assume a kneeling, at-attention position after you offer your thanks."

Hoping she understood him correctly, Julianna knelt back on her haunches, trying to hold herself so her ass barely grazed her heels, the tender skin still throbbing from the caning. Shaking back her hair, she lifted her arms and locked her fingers behind her head. She gazed straight ahead, fervently wishing Stephen and his henchmen would suddenly disappear in a burst of flame, or better yet, that she'd awaken from this horrible nightmare.

Instead Stephen gestured to the men, jerking his head toward the door. They walked out of the hut, but remained just outside the open door. Stephen turned to Julianna. "Who are you?"

Julianna drew a breath. "Number thirty-eight."

He struck her cheek and she instinctively reached for her face with a cry. He struck her again. "Back into position! Never fall out of position. Now we'll try it again. And this time address me properly!"

With tears in her eyes, Julianna managed to reassume the position, hands behind her head. "Who are you?" he said again.

"Number thirty-eight…sir."

"That's correct. And what are you?"

Julianna stared at him blankly. Had he told her this? What she was, or rather, what he wanted her to say she was? She racked her brain, and could recall nothing about this. He was watching her, his eyes hard, his mouth curving into a cruel smile. He lifted his hand and suddenly she remembered and said breathlessly, "A worthless slave, sir!"

His hand dropped to his side. "That's right. Right now all you are is a worthless slave. But we will teach you, number thirty-eight. You will be stripped of your modesty and your pride. You will learn to serve in ways that never even crossed your innocent, narrow little mind. We will mold you until you are no longer worthless, but very valuable indeed. You will become a sex slave, a pain slut, an eager whore. I'll teach you all about the masochistic pleasure of a thorough whipping while your Master's cock is shoved down your pretty little throat.

"In the final stage of your training, you will do more than merely submit. You will come to embrace your new status. You will live for your orgasm. You will die inside each time you disappoint, and you will pay the consequences, rest assured. You will exalt in your degradation, and thank us for each and every new humiliation."

He stared down at her, a fire behind his eyes. "Not only that, you will mean it. It is that sincerity I seek. That sincerity I demand. It is not enough to merely go through the motions, pretending to be obedient, while inside your defiance rages."

Julianna looked down at hearing these words, wondering if her expression had given her away. Stephen laughed softly. "Not only is your body—every inch, every hole—now in our possession, but your mind is as well. I will break you down, number thirty-eight, not to destroy you, but to build you back into something worth a great deal to men willing to pay for it."

He put his finger under her chin, forcing her to look up. "I am not easy to fool. I will know when you have truly succumbed to my power, and accepted and embraced your new role as slave. Then, and only then, will you be ready for sale. How long we keep you here, and where you ultimately end up, is up to you."

He moved behind her. "Stand up. Let me see the welts." Julianna rose unsteadily to her feet, forcing herself to get into position. Mercifully, the cramps in her gut had eased somewhat. Stephen ran a finger along one welt, his touch rough against the tender skin. He put his mouth close to her ear. "This is nothing, number thirty-eight, nothing to the beating you will receive if you try to defy or disobey me or any of the trainers or guards."

He moved back to face her. "This is a business. Time is money. If I decide you're taking too long to make the transition, then instead of finding yourself in the palace of some Middle Eastern sheik, or the country estate of some British Earl, you will be sold to pimps who will whore you out to any taker with a wad of cash stuffed in their pants. You'll be lucky if you live out the year in their clutches."

Julianna's legs gave out and she sank to the floor. She felt too weak and frightened to move. Stephen continued above her, "I trust you've learned your lesson, number thirty-eight. Don't prove me wrong."

She heard the door close and the piece of wood that kept her locked in being dropped into place but she didn't move. Only when she heard the vehicle engine start up and then fade away did she lift her head and push herself upright.

She looked around the small hut, hardly able to believe this was really happening, though the welts on her ass and thighs felt all too real. She stood slowly, glad that the dizziness caused from hunger had abated, though the stomachache she'd traded for it wasn't much better.

She touched the abraded lines that crisscrossed her skin. Twisting back, she tried to see the damage. She was shocked to see the dark red lines and began to feel faint again. At the same time, her damn intestines were acting up, and she knew she'd have no choice but to use the bucket.

She'd had to pee during the night, and had torn a piece of the now useless dress to use as toilet paper. Moving toward the cot, she tore another piece of the gauzy fabric and took it with her to the waste bucket, dreading the thought of having to squat and defecate over it.

She placed a leg on either side of the bucket and lowered herself, careful not to touch it as she willed her bowels to release and ease the painful cramps. She glanced at the camera in the ceiling, her face turning hot at the thought of some creep watching her, but she had no choice. Her bodily needs finally won out over her embarrassment. She wiped herself as best she could and dropped the soiled piece of fabric into the bucket. She draped the remainder of the dress over the bucket, though it did little to block the stink in the small, windowless hut.

She moved back to the cot and lay down on her stomach, trying not to dwell on what new horrors lay in her future. To think, only a few days before she'd thought that finally something good was happening, that her luck was turning around. What a joke. She'd been set up from start to finish. This whole thing was organized, funded and executed with cold precision and detachment. A business, Stephen had said, that dealt in slave trafficking.

Not only that, they intended to brainwash her. She was no longer Julianna Beckett. She was a number, an object, to be molded, sold, used and discarded. She shivered, though the room was warm, and rolled to her side, hugging herself.

"You are not a number," she said softly, the microphones be damned. "You are Julianna Beckett, daughter of Emily Anne Beckett, and you will survive this."

Emily Anne...the proud, strong woman who had raised her daughter alone, always her protector and later as Julianna matured, her friend as well. And then last year the cancer hit, striking like a snake, sinking its venomous fangs fatally into her. Mother became daughter as Emily was left as weak, bald and helpless as a baby, ravaged by both the cancer and its treatment. Yet even through it all, her mother's spirit never wavered.

Don't let them break your spirit, Alma had whispered. Julianna could hear her mother's voice in her head, echoing these words.

Julianna would fight. She had no weapons and she was a prisoner on this tiny island in the middle of nowhere, with no apparent way out. Nevertheless, she wouldn't give up. She would fight, with stealth and cunning, until she found a way to escape. There was no other tenable choice.

The idea of being subjugated, her free will denied, her liberty stolen, her very essence as a human being *erased,* was simply not an option. She would get away, come hell or high water. She would do it for Emily.

She would do it for herself.

Chapter 4

Julianna was lying on her cot when they came through the door. She sat up and hunched her knees to her chest, wrapping her arms around them as the two guards who had beaten her came into the hut. She tensed, terrified it was going to happen again.

"Get up. It's time to go," one of them said in English, though his accent sounded Spanish. She was at once relieved and anxious. What new torture awaited her? The man who spoke was swarthy, with black eyes, a broad nose and very tan skin. The other man had fairer skin, dusted with freckles, his hair a rusty red. He had a pointy nose and chin, and reminded her of a fox.

So, you can talk, she wanted to say, but didn't. No point in antagonizing the men who had beaten her twice and had been given the right to rape her. She stood nervously, covering her body awkwardly with her arms, though neither man seemed to look at her with much interest.

The dark man, who she dubbed the Spaniard in her head, produced two sets of Velcro cuffs with clips attached. He placed them on her wrists and ankles, securing the wrist cuffs behind her back. The other man, the one she would call Fox, attached a short piece of chain between the ankle cuffs, hobbling her but leaving enough room to walk.

They led her out of the hot, stinking hut and Julianna breathed deeply, grateful to be in the open air. "Where are you taking me?" she dared.

"Slave quarters," the Spaniard replied tersely. They placed her between them on the ATV and drove toward the center of the island, stopping in front of the barracks she had seen before. As they took her from the vehicle, she couldn't stop trembling.

They led her through a door on the side of the building and entered a long, narrow corridor with barred cells along either side. Julianna looked to her right and left as she was hustled down the hall. She counted eight cells, four on each side. Each had a mattress set in an iron frame and a toilet in the corner. In three of the cells she saw naked women, each curled on her bed, apparently asleep. They all had thick leather collars around their necks, with a chain running from the collar to the iron leg of the bedstead. One of them was facing the wall as she slept, and Julianna saw that her back and ass were covered with long, thin red welts much like the ones now fading on her own body.

She jumped and drew in her breath sharply at the sound of a woman's screams somewhere farther down the corridor. Neither the Spaniard nor Fox seemed to notice, or if they did, they ignored it. They led her past the cells to a much larger area that had three showerheads set into the wall, and two long, thick black hoses coiled beneath them. There were drains in the floor and Julianna realized it was some kind of communal shower.

She expected to be told to shower. She knew she stank from sweat and being confined in that stifling, rank space for so many hours, and her hair was a tangled mess. She longed for the fresh, clean water and the feel of soap lathering on her skin.

But instead of leading her to the showers, the men led her to the adjoining wall. It had eyebolts of varying sizes and thicknesses embedded into it. Fox released the clips that held her arms behind her but then re-clipped them together in front of her. He raised her wrists and attached the clips to one of the bolts. Reaching down, he removed the cuffs and chain from her ankles and set them aside.

"What are you doing? Please, don't hurt me."

Neither man responded. They both went to a large table with supplies on it and put on thick rubber aprons. Fox moved toward the wall and picked up one of the coiled black hoses. The Spaniard selected a scrub brush with a long handle from the supply table. He squeezed a generous amount of liquid soap onto it.

Fox pressed the handle of the metal nozzle at the end of the hose and water began to spray from it, and Julianna understood she was to be hosed down again. Fox turned the jet of water on her. It was cold and she gasped, sputtered and twisted as the water sprayed over her body and face.

The Spaniard used the scrub brush, soaping her skin from head to toe, turning her this way and that as he cleaned her. "Spread your legs," he said at one point, pushing the brush between her thighs and rubbing it over her pussy and between her ass cheeks while she squeezed her eyes closed. He even washed her hair, using his hands instead of the brush, while Fox stood by, ready to rinse.

The Spaniard finally let her down, pulling the wet cuffs from her wrists, while Fox re-coiled the hose and returned it to its place. "Arms out." The Spaniard began to towel her dry. Apparently she didn't move quickly enough. Before she could obey, Fox moved behind her and forcibly held her arms out on either side of her body.

When they were done manhandling her, she was led to a low metal table that was tilted upward on one end, the two front legs higher than the rear. Fox pointed and said, "Lie down, knees bent, legs spread, feet flat on either side of your body."

It was the first time he had spoken in her presence. His accent was American. For a terrified moment she thought he was going to rape her in that peculiar but very exposed position. Instead she was surprised by a warm washcloth being draped over her spread sex. She soon realized when the Spaniard returned holding a razor and a can of shaving cream what their intentions were.

She squeezed her eyes shut as one of the men pushed her thighs farther apart and held them open while the other squirted shaving cream over her sex and began to draw the razor over the skin. He was surprisingly gentle, for which she was silently grateful. When he was done, they shaved her legs and underarms, working quickly and efficiently. She found herself wondering how many women they had done this to before.

While the Spaniard put things away, Fox produced a large comb, running it through Julianna's hair, his eyes flitting over her face. The lack of emotion the two men displayed was even more disconcerting in a way than Stephen's anger or Vince's slobbering leers. How long had they been doing this, to have become so inured to what they were taking part in?

Still naked, she was led back down the corridor to an empty cell. Fox unlocked the narrow, barred door and pulled it open. The Spaniard pushed Julianna in ahead of him. "Time to eat," he said, nodding toward Fox. At the mention of eating, Julianna's stomach instantly leaped awake. Fox left the cell, hopefully to get her meal. The Spaniard sat on the bed and pointed at the ground.

"Kneel at attention."

Julianna obeyed, the thought of food spurring her on as much as his thickly-muscled arms and torso. She laced her fingers behind her head and waited in the silence. She could still hear the woman's cries somewhere in the distance, and her heart ached with helpless sympathy.

She stole a glance at the Spaniard, who was staring at her without expression. She was hungry and exhausted, and her arms ached in their position behind her head, but she didn't dare lower them. Not with the possible promise of food in the offing.

A few minutes later Fox returned and he was indeed carrying a tray that contained two bowls. He set it down on the floor in front of Julianna. One bowl contained water. The other held rice, beans and sausage, the same food that had been offered and then denied by Stephen. Julianna swore to herself she would get the food this time, no matter what she had to do to earn it.

"Slaves are fed, or they eat by themselves. Which do you want?" the Spaniard asked.

What a stupid question, Julianna thought, but aloud she said, "By myself, please, sir."

The Spaniard nodded, something like a smile moving briefly over his face. He looked at Fox, who Julianna saw was also smiling, and she gulped, certain she'd just stumbled into a carefully laid trap. The Spaniard stood and pulled something from one of the large pockets on the leg of his pants. She saw it was another set of the Velcro cuffs. "Hands behind your back," he said.

"But, you said—"

"Hands behind your back," he repeated.

Confused, Julianna obeyed. How could she eat without the use of her hands? She realized there were no utensils beside the bowl of food.

The Spaniard clipped her wrists together and then gathered her wet hair in one hand. Using the hair itself, he tied it into a loose knot at the back of her neck. He placed his hand on her upper back and pushed her down toward the food. "Eat."

Julianna struggled to keep her balance as he pushed her. "What? I don't understand."

But she did understand. These fuckers were expecting her to eat like an animal, using her mouth and rooting in the bowl while they watched. The thought at once enraged and humiliated her, but she was too hungry to care at this point, and knew any protest would be useless.

These two guys were servants, nothing more. They were performing their duties with disinterest, even indifference. They didn't care if she ate or not. They probably didn't care if she lived or died. *They* were the animals, not her.

She leaned forward, blinking away tears of frustration and anger as she lowered her face to the food. She touched it with her tongue and found it was only warm, not too hot. She licked at it, managing to scoop some of the rice and beans into her mouth, but only a little.

The taste of the food awakened her thirst. She leaned forward again, at first trying to lick at the water in the bowl, which wasn't too successful. She quickly figured out it worked much better to suck up the water with pursed lips, and she was able to drink her fill.

She saw in her peripheral vision that both men were now seated on the bed, thighs touching. Fox's hand, she noticed, was resting lightly on the Spaniard's knee. She was too distracted by the tantalizing food in front of her to pay much attention to them, however.

Turning back to the food, she lowered her face farther into the bowl and, using her lips and teeth, this time got a good mouthful of the delicious food. She couldn't help the moan of sheer pleasure as she chewed.

It was hard to eat this way, holding her body over the bowl, her arms cuffed behind her back. The bowl kept shifting, clinking into the water bowl or sliding to the edge of the tray as she struggled to get a mouthful. She tried to block out the men watching her as if she was a dog on display.

After a while she worked herself into a kind of rhythm, using her tongue to scoop up what she could and then closing her lips over the food before it fell back into the bowl. She ate as fast as she could, not sure how much of the food she would be permitted. She knew she would probably suffer another stomachache after this, but it would be worth it to have something substantial in her belly.

To her relief and surprise, they actually let her finish all the food. She again tackled the water bowl, slurping up mouthfuls. Finally she sat back. Fox pulled a bandana from his back pocket and wiped a bit of rice from her cheek. She felt as helpless as an infant.

"Use the toilet before we go," the Spaniard said.

"Please, sir, how am I supposed to do it?" Julianna twisted her back toward them to remind them she was cuffed. She did in fact have to pee, but surely they didn't mean for her to do it with her hands behind her back, and with them watching. No way in hell was she going to poop in front of them. She could already feel her intestines shutting down in protest.

"You need to go, you figure it out." He shrugged, adding, "Hurry up. The trainer is waiting." At those words, Julianna's stomach contracted with fear. The Spaniard stood and moved toward her, gripping her beneath one arm and pulling her to her feet. Directing her toward the metal commode, he forced her down onto it.

"I can't—" she began.

The Spaniard cut her off by placing two fingers her lips. "Do it. You'll be sorry later if you miss your chance." She knew he was right and realized she should be grateful to him, in a weird way, for his insistence.

She tried to get her body to relax enough to release the urine from her bladder with the two men in the cell. They were both watching her, their expressions indifferent. Closing her eyes, Julianna imagined water running from a faucet and willed herself to let go.

Thankfully she managed to do it, the urine splashing into the water, the sound echoing in the small cell and amplifying her humiliation. She saw the roll of toilet paper on the floor beside the toilet. "Please, can you release my hands so I can wipe myself, sir?"

Fox reached for the toilet paper and tore off a few squares. Julianna's humiliation was complete when he reached between her legs and wiped her. They pulled her from the seat and took her out of the cell into the corridor. They went past the shower and in the direction of the screaming, though now all was silent.

Suddenly she realized why. It was her turn.

They opened the last door on the left, and Julianna found herself in what looked like some kind of lab, with an examination table like the kind a gynecologist would have, and lots of strange metal and leather tools on a counter that spanned the full length of one of the walls.

Stephen stepped out from behind a tall screen in the corner of the room, wiping his hands on a towel. "Ah, there you are. Right on time." He nodded at the men. "Strap her on the table and you may go."

"No, no, no!" Julianna struggled against the strong men holding her, but she was no match for them. They easily hoisted her onto the metal exam table. Releasing her cuffs, they forced her to lie down, and then set about securing thick leather straps over her midriff and across her hips. They reattached her wrist cuffs to hooks set into the sides of the table and then pushed her legs up, forcing them wide open as they buckled her feet into the stirrups at the end of the table and secured her thighs to the legs of the stirrups with additional leather bands.

"No, you can't do this!" she protested vainly, as she struggled and fought. The men ignored her, handling her as if she were an inanimate object as they focused on their task of restraining her. In less than a minute she was bound and spread, completely exposed to the trainer, not to mention the Spaniard and Fox. Once done, they left the room, closing the door behind them.

Stephen approached the side of the table, his eyes flashing beneath furrowed brows. "Of course we can do this. We can do whatever we want. The sooner you figure that out, the better off you'll be." He smacked her cheek with his open palm several times, very hard. Tears sprang to her eyes as she gasped with pain. "You are a stupid girl. We shall have to work extra hard to penetrate," he slapped her again, "that thick," and again, "skull of yours."

Gripping her by the throat just below her jaw, he effectively cut off her ability to breathe. She could feel the pressure building in her face and a deep panic roiling in her gut. She opened her mouth, trying to gasp for air, to beg him to let her go, but no sound could pass the viselike grip on her trachea.

Her lungs burned and her eyes began to flutter shut. "Open your eyes! Look at me. Don't stop looking at me." Julianna opened her eyes, wondering through the pounding in her head if this was it—the way she would die. She kept her eyes on his, noticing the darker gray circle around the almost silver gray irises. He was leaning so close she could see each individual dark eyelash. They were beautiful eyes, she found herself thinking, in a cruel, hard face.

"I control your breath. Your life is literally in my hands. Do you understand?"

She couldn't reply, save for a slight nod. He stared down at her, the anger easing from his face until he almost smiled. Finally he let her go and she drew in a deep, grateful breath of air, her lungs expanding in relief.

In his deep, sonorous voice, Stephen asked, "Who are you?"

She stared at him, her mind blank, her heart beating over-fast against her ribs. He reached for her throat again and her mind clicked on. "Number thirty-eight, sir," she lied.

He stood upright, dropping his hand. "That's right. And what are you?"

"A...a worthless slave...sir."

"Say it again, with more conviction." He touched her throat with two fingers.

"A worthless slave, sir!"

"That's correct." Stepping away from her, he moved from her line of sight. When he returned, he had donned a white lab coat over his clothing. He took a pair of latex gloves from the pocket and put them on, flexing his fingers in front of her, a cruel smile on his face. With the coat, the gloves and the wild look in his eye, he gave the impression of a mad scientist. It would have been almost funny if it weren't so terrifying. She was alone in the torture chamber of a madman, strapped down to a table, completely at his mercy. She bit her lip so hard she could taste blood.

Turning toward the counter, he selected something and turned back to her. He moved to stand between her legs. "It's time for your examination." He held up a stainless steel speculum, its large blunt blades in the shape of a duck's bill. Julianna gasped, crying out in fear as she struggled in vain against her restraints.

With an evil smile, he took a tube of lubricant from the counter and smeared the rounded edges of the speculum blades with it. He crouched down between her legs. She startled and squealed as the cold, gooey tips of the blades were inserted into her. Despite his admonitions to relax, her body was rigid with fear, her muscles clamping down painfully on the speculum blades as they were pushed slowly into her.

When they were fully inside her, he said, "Now, I'm going to widen the speculum. I suggest you remain as still as you can. I wouldn't want to hurt you, at least not by accident." He chuckled. She felt the blades widening inside her as he turned the wheel to spread them. Never especially comfortable with this kind of examination at the doctor's office, the circumstances in this psychopath's torture chamber magnified the discomfort a thousand-fold.

Stephen pulled a penlight from his lab coat pocket and shone the beam on her spread pussy. "Healthy pink tissue," he remarked clinically. "Strong vaginal muscles, perfect for pleasing a man. You shall fetch a pretty penny with that tight little cunt of yours." Julianna closed her eyes, tears of humiliation and rage trickling into her hair. Finally he pulled the offending object from her. She was dying to slam her legs shut, but she couldn't move an inch.

Stephen dropped the speculum into a sink set at the end of the counter and returned to her, his hands still gloved. "Time for your anal inspection." Julianna gasped as he pushed a finger into her ass and then a second one, twisting them painfully inside her.

As she cried out, he murmured, "Excellent. An anal virgin. Jason will like that." He snickered as he continued to probe and stretch her while a stream of curses hurtled through her mind. Finally he let her alone, withdrawing the offending fingers and moving back toward the sink, where he stripped off the gloves.

He returned to stand beside her, his eyes moving over her naked body, violating her with his insolent, predatory gaze. If she could have broken through her bonds, she would have leaped from the table and strangled the bastard with her bare hands.

He ran his hands lightly over her breasts, cupping them, thumbs and forefingers closing over the nipples. He rolled them until they stiffened. Leaning over her, he bared his teeth and caught her right nipple in between them. She gasped with fear, though he wasn't really hurting her—yet. He did the same with the left nipple and then replaced teeth with tongue, licking in circles around the engorged nipples, which, once wet, hardened further in the cool air of the room.

He stood again by the side of the table, running his hands down her sides, over her stomach and along her legs. He prodded and pinched her muscles, handling her as if she was a horse or show dog.

Stepping to the counter, he returned with a long black wand with a fat, spongy-looking ball at its end. As he flicked the switch at its base, it began to hum, the ball vibrating. He smiled at her. "You know what this is, eh? Of course you do." She was pretty sure she did know, but she didn't reply.

He flicked off the vibrator and moved to stand between her legs. Kneeling, he brought his face close to her spread, bared sex. Bound flat as she was, he was now out of her range of vision. She felt him tug at her labia, pulling and stretching her. She squeaked in fear as a finger pressed its way inside her. She tensed as he probed her.

He continued to move his finger, adding a second and then withdrawing them to glide over her labia and the hood of her clit. She realized she wasn't breathing and her bound hands were clenched tight, her fingernails digging into her palms. He stood and she could hear the motor's hum again as he turned on the vibrator. She jerked in her restraints as the pulsing head made contact with her pussy.

At first it just kind of tickled. She squirmed and tried to twist away from the vibration, but she was held fast in her restraints. He moved it over her labia, pressing lightly against her clit. She could feel her body responding, despite being tied down and despite her fear. The tickle moved into something more urgent. She began to breathe harder, unable to help herself as the machine stimulated her clit, which was throbbing against it.

"You think you're going to come, thirty-eight?" He moved the vibrator in a slow, steady circle over her sex.

"I—I, yes," she gasped, a part of her horrified with herself, though she couldn't control her body's reaction to the relentless stimulation.

"No." He pulled the rubber ball away and Julianna felt her muscles ease, though her clit still throbbed. "You won't come, until I tell you to. If you do, you'll be punished." He replaced the spongy head against her sex, now moving it in tight circles directly over her clit. The pressure began to mount again, even more quickly than before.

Julianna felt her body shaking. She was furious with herself for responding to this horrible man's touch, but she couldn't help it. The vibrator was too stimulating and she had no way to resist it. He had to let her come. She tried to lift her head, straining against the collar around her throat and nearly choking herself in the process. "Please! Please, I have to... Can I, uh, may I come, sir?" She was panting, her body rigid, the orgasm nearly upon her.

"No." He didn't let up. "Don't come or you'll be punished."

She tried to steel herself against the vibrator, willing her body not to come. She squeezed her eyes shut and clenched every muscle in her vain effort to resist. If only he'd take the damn thing off her! How the hell was she supposed to obey him when he made it impossible for her to do so?

"Ah, god," she finally moaned, helpless as the vibrator wrenched a throbbing climax from her unwilling body. She strained hard against the leather bindings as a long, powerful orgasm was wrested from her. She whimpered as he continued to move the rubber head against her, pulling a second orgasm right on the heels of the first.

The sensation was too much, moving just past pleasure into something more like pain. "Please! You have to stop. You have to..." Then a curious thing began to happen. The pain eased its way back into a pulsing stroke of pleasure. She could feel her clit, swollen and throbbing beneath the relentless vibration of the sex toy. She was panting, her body bathed in sweat, her heart beating a mad tattoo against her bones.

"Please!" she gasped, no longer sure what she was asking for, as she came yet again.

Finally, mercifully, the motor's hum was flicked off, the only sound in the room her own ragged breathing. She lay limp in her bonds, her mind empty, drifting in a kind of semi-conscious haze.

His voice tore through the sexual reverie. "You came, you naughty, naughty girl. Now you will be punished." He was again at her side, staring down at her with those cold gray eyes.

"But I couldn't—"

"Silence!" he said sharply. "No excuses. You break the rules, you pay the price. End of discussion."

It was so unfair! He'd forced her to come. He'd given her no choice. It wasn't as if she could control her body, not when he used that thing on her. He'd done it on purpose, the bastard. He knew exactly what he was doing.

As if reading her thoughts, he said, "You will learn to control your orgasms, thirty-eight. You will obey your Master over your own body. *He* will control your behavior and reaction, not your own filthy little cunt. Do I make myself clear?"

No, you asshole. Fuck you. "Yes, sir," she managed through teeth clenched with rage. He wasn't really asking her anything. He was telling her how things would be. Somehow she had to learn to deal on his terms or suffer the consequences. Shit, either way she'd suffer the consequences, as the whole game was rigged from the start.

He offered a small, cold smile. "Good girl. Now you'll have your punishment, as you deserve." He turned toward the counter lined with nefarious-looking objects. Turning back to her, he held up two small rectangular pads with wires coming out the ends. "Are you familiar with electrical stimulation? It can be a most effective reminder to behave."

He stepped around the table until he was standing between her knees. Julianna tried to keep her panic at bay. "Please. Don't hurt me. I'll be good. I promise," she begged.

"Oh yes, you will. I'll see to it," he replied. She lifted her head, ignoring the cut of the collar at her throat as she struggled to see what he was doing. Using the hem of his lab coat, he wiped the remaining lubricant from her pussy lips. Pulling the protective paper from one side of the electrode pads, he pressed the sticky adhesive side to her outer labia. Returning to the counter, he held up a shiny black phallus for her to see. It also had wires trailing from its base, plugged into a small black box with switches and dials. He moved back between her legs. Julianna began to shake.

"Please," she begged. "Don't do this. Don't hurt me."

"I don't recall speaking directly to you, so there's no reason for you to be speaking. Must I gag you?"

Julianna didn't answer.

"A direct question, number thirty-eight."

"No, sir," she replied in a tiny voice.

"Some women find this procedure quite, ah, pleasurable, though admittedly at lower voltage levels than I plan to use on you." Julianna felt a slight tug at the electrode pads adhering to her labia and realized he must be plugging those wires in as well. Then she felt the large phallus being inserted into her pussy. She tensed against the invasion, shuddering as the hard, thick phallus stretched her open.

"Electro-stimulation," he continued in a detached voice, as if lecturing in a classroom, "is interesting as a torture device, as there are no signs that will give away what to expect. Usually when one inflicts pain with, say, a whip or a cane, it's possible for the recipient to anticipate what is coming and somehow prepare. While with electroshock, you don't know what's coming, when."

A zing of painful current suddenly ripped its way through Julianna's pussy. Her muscles clamped down against the phallus. She screamed and arched against the leather straps holding her down and open. Sweat beaded on her forehead and slicked beneath her body on the metal table. Stephen continued speaking as if nothing had happened. "This device stimulates your nerve endings using a carefully produced electrical signal. It can be pleasurable at lower settings. Or it can be quite painful."

Julianna screamed again as a powerful jolt moved through her pussy. "Stop! Please!" she gasped.

"Take it. You earned it. You deserve it." Again Julianna was shocked from the inside out, and again she screamed.

The process continued, with him zapping her in no predictable pattern. After a while she no longer heard what he was saying over the beating of her heart and her own screams. Every muscle in her body was rigid with anticipation. Sweat covered her body as she trembled and jerked with each new shock.

When he finally stopped, she lay exhausted and panting, only dimly aware as he removed the phallus and electrodes from her sex. Her legs fell limply to the table when he unbuckled them from the stirrups.

Releasing the leather bands that held her in place and unchaining her wrists, Stephen dragged her from the table, catching her as she fell forward and pressing her to the floor. "Thank me."

Afraid of what he might do next if she disobeyed, Julianna forced herself to kneel at his feet. The memory of the electroshock still pulsed in her pussy but she realized with relief she had suffered no real harm. She bent forward and kissed his shoe. "Thank you, sir—" She took a deep, ragged breath, forcing herself to continue. "—for using this worthless slave."

"You're welcome." He stepped back. She stayed where she was, eyes down.

"Okay, Vince," Stephen added. "You can have her for about fifteen minutes. Then take her to Anders."

Chapter 5

Julianna's head jerked up. When had that asshole come into the room? Vince stood just inside the door, the erection in his shorts clearly visible.

At Stephen's words, Vince moved toward her, expertly grabbing and cuffing her wrists behind her back before she had a chance to react. He pulled her to her feet, jerking her by the O-ring on her collar. Grabbing her arm in a tight grip, he hauled her from the room.

"Have fun," Stephen called out, his dry laugh echoing in Julianna's ears as Vince pulled her down the hall.

Vince forced her into a room that held a bed with a small table beside it that held a large box of condoms. He released her cuffs, but only to throw her down onto the mattress. He wasted no time pulling off his shorts, his long, thin cock fully erect above heavy, hairy balls. He tore at a packet and slid a condom over his shaft while Julianna cowered on the bed.

"My turn, bitch," he snarled, falling on top of her as she struggled to get away from him.

He reared up over her, gripping her wrists painfully and wrenching them over her head as he pressed his sheathed cock inside her. She screamed and he released one wrist long enough to slap her face. "Shut up and take what's coming to you, cunt. This'll teach you to kick the family jewels."

He rutted inside her, hurting tender tissue already bruised from the speculum and the electroshock, despite the lubricant left over from the phallus. Fortunately, he only lasted maybe three minutes before shuddering and jerking into a climax as he grunted like a pig. He slid off her and lay beside her for a minute, apparently catching his breath. She curled away from him, closing her eyes as she rocked herself.

She heard Vince moving and felt him rise from the bed. "Get on the floor and thank me, bitch."

Julianna rolled to the floor and knelt, touching his sandal-clad foot with her lips. "Thank you, sir," she managed to push through clenched teeth.

He shoved his foot upward against her mouth. "Go on. You didn't say it all."

"...for using this worthless slave, sir," she added, hating him with a fierce, raw passion.

"You're welcome, cunt. There's a lot more where that came from." He stepped back and pulled up his shorts, dropping the used condom in a plastic trashcan beside the door.

"You can wait here for Anders. I'd stay longer, but I've got things to do, places to go."

Crimes to commit, women to rape, she wanted to add, but held her tongue. He shut the door behind him and she heard the turning of the lock. Wearily she climbed back onto the bed, wondering who the hell Anders was, and if he could possibly be any more loathsome than either Stephen or Vince.

~*~

"Open your eyes, Julianna."

At the use of her name, Julianna's eyes sprang open. Standing over her was a tall man in his late twenties with broad shoulders and thick, straight blond hair falling into the bluest eyes she had ever seen. His nose was narrow and curved down like an eagle's beak. He smiled at her, showing square white teeth against the red of his sensuous lips.

She hadn't even realized she'd fallen asleep, though it couldn't have been for very long. "My name is Anders. I am one of your trainers." Julianna turned her head away, suppressing a groan. "Can you stand?" His tone was so solicitous. She turned back to face him and found herself nodding.

He waited as she hauled herself upright. Her pussy felt raw and sore and she wanted to cry, but she forced back the tears, pressing her lips together. Anders put his arm around her and she didn't dare shrug him off, though she wanted to.

"You are tired," he said gently. "Come with me." Anders led her to a room two doors down from the torture exam room. This room also contained a bed, but it was much more sumptuous, piled with plump white pillows over a dark blue satin quilt. One wall was covered entirely with mirrors. Anders directed Julianna to sit on the bed. She saw herself reflected in the mirrored wall, looking pale and fragile, dark smudges beneath her eyes, her mouth drawn down in a frown. She turned away.

Anders moved toward a corner of the room where there was a sink and turned on the water. She stared at his broad back, wondering what would happen next. He seemed so different from everyone else on this wretched island, but was he? Or was this just the velvet exterior covering an iron fist. She shuddered and hugged herself, waiting.

He returned with a basin and a washcloth. Setting the basin on the floor beside the bed, he dipped the cloth in, ringing it out. "Lie down in the center of the bed," he said. Too exhausted to ponder what new trap was being laid for her, she fell back against the pillows, the soft satin cushioning her body. Anders brought the washcloth to her face and Julianna smelled lavender and lemon. The cloth was warm and soft against her skin as he gently washed her face and neck. He dipped the cloth again and began to wash her body. The water was warm and felt wonderful on her skin. He washed her as if she were an invalid or a small child, moving slowly over her limbs and torso, wiping away the sweat and the filthy touch of both Stephen and Vince.

He was so tender, so gentle, and she was so tired—physically and emotionally exhausted from the physical privations and tortures, as well as her constant fear. Tears began to well in her eyes and spill over. He noticed and touched her cheek, tracking a tear as it fell. "Crying can be a good thing," he said. "It purifies the soul." He wasn't American, though his English was perfect—almost too perfect, the vowels round and clear, the consonants enunciated.

When he spread her legs, panic pushed its way through her, the electroshock and Vince's rape both still sharp and raw in her body and mind. But even there his touch was gentle and careful, running the warm, soapy cloth gently over her labia and down between her cheeks. Through it all, Julianna was passive as a baby, the trauma of her ordeal overcoming her as she lay limp in the soft, comfortable bed, being ministered to with such seeming tenderness.

He patted her dry and applied a soothing lotion to her skin, rubbing it in slow easy circles over her body. He combed her hair back with his fingers and tucked it behind her ears. "Your hair is an extraordinary color of coppery red, nearly golden where the light hits it. And your eyes, clear green glass, with gold flecks like the sun."

Despite herself, Julianna liked these compliments, though she was deeply wary as to their real intent. Was he setting her up for some kind of fall? She found herself both grateful and thoroughly confused by how he was treating her—was it just a trick to lull her into complacency before the next terrifying torture took place?

He rose from the bed, looking down at her with eyes that seemed almost kind. "Do you feel better now?"

"Yes," she admitted. She realized she hadn't said the requisite *sir* at the end of her sentence and she tensed, waiting to be reprimanded, but no rebuke came. Instead

Anders lay on the bed beside her, gliding his hand under her shoulder and pulling her toward him.

She lay flat on her back, rigid beside him. "Relax." His voice was soothing. "You are tired. Rest." He was lying on his side, one arm still beneath her shoulders. With the other he began to trace the curve of her breast, moving his fingers in slow circles around her nipple. She shuddered and drew in her breath, but didn't dare push him away.

"Your breasts are perfection," he murmured. "The nipples are the color of rose petals against the cream of your skin." She almost smiled at his flowery language. Who the hell was this guy? He leaned over, placing his mouth on her nipple, sucking lightly at it and circling it with his tongue. His touch, unlike Stephen's, was gentle, even sensual.

When he lifted his head, the nipple had hardened, its color deepening as it engorged with blood. Julianna found herself both ashamed and aroused by his touch. It was like sleeping with the enemy. It was one thing to submit, quite another to enjoy. Yet when he dipped his head again, this time licking and teasing the other nipple with equal skill and tenderness, it too responded to his touch.

He smiled. "You please me. I sense a deep sensuality in you. We will explore that together, you and I." He ran his hand over her skin, moving down her torso and stroking her stomach. Finally his hand rested over her pubic mound. She stiffened again, pressing her thighs tight and turning her head away.

"You are frightened," he said softly. "I understand." He continued to cup her sex with his hand. "Look at me." Slowly she turned her head, forcing herself to open her eyes. "I want you to relax your muscles. Let your legs fall open. I know you are shy and this situation is difficult for you, but you must obey me."

Shy? Did this man suffer from the delusion she was here of her own volition? That they were on some kind of weird blind date where you got naked first and talked after? *Difficult?* Try fucking terrifying!

"Ah, you are angry, I can see it in your face." He shook his head, smiling. "Anger has no place in your life anymore. Let go of that anger. It will be so much easier for you." He moved his hand to her thigh, pressing his fingers between her closed legs. His hand was strong and she was afraid to resist much more. She let her thighs part.

He stroked her outer labia with a light touch, his fingers dancing over the area recently subjected to Stephen's cruel treatment. She closed her eyes and pressed her lips together. "Uncurl your fists," he said. She hadn't realized they were clenched. "Stop fighting me."

I'll never stop fighting, she vowed silently, but she forced her hands to relax. He continued to stroke and tease her sex, his hand moving slowly inward and down. He touched her entrance gently, not with the brutish invasion Stephen had employed. Carefully he eased a finger inside her. Julianna tensed and tried to close her legs but Anders stopped her, a sternness entering his voice for the first time. "No. You will not resist me. I will not permit it."

He began to probe again, as careful and gentle as before. Despite her fear and distress, her body began to react to his touch, the muscles loosening, the dry tissue moistening at the stimulation. He withdrew the finger and slid it up over her labia, moving in a light swirl. He came near but didn't touch her hooded clit, instead running a teasing circle around it until, despite herself, she began to want that touch. The finger moved down, entering her again. This time it slid in easily and she felt him pressing a second one in beside the first.

He did something then with his fingers, touching something inside that made her jerk and gasp, "Oh!" The sensation was at once strange and deeply arousing. She couldn't deny it, despite the situation in which she found herself.

"Yes," he murmured. "That's it. Let yourself go. Give yourself fully to the sensations." He continued to move his fingers inside her, and each time he touched that strange sweet spot she jerked and gasped. When he finally withdrew his fingers, they were slick with her juices as he slid them, held together in a boy scout's salute, over her inner labia. When they made contact with her clit, a soft moan slipped from Julianna's lips. Her nipples were erect and she felt a flush creeping over her neck and cheeks.

She was angry with her body for betraying her by responding to his touch, but at the same time it felt so good. Unlike the fast, hard orgasms the vibrator had pulled from her, this was slow and gentle, like the warm lazy currents of a river on a summer's day, lulling and soothing her into pleasure. Why should she deny herself? Maybe she should seize this tiny respite, offered in the face of the continuing terror that awaited her.

He continued to move his fingers over and around her clit, his touch light as butterfly wings. Slowly he increased the pressure against her now throbbing clit. It was just right, the perfect blend of friction and swirl. "Oh god," she groaned, the words bypassing her brain. She began to pant, the buttery hot sensation of an impending orgasm moving in radiating waves from her pussy throughout her body.

"Yes," he murmured, his mouth close to her ear, his breath smelling of cloves. "Give yourself to me." He dipped his head, his lips closing over her nipple as his fingers continued their relentless, perfect dance on her sex.

She began to tremble and then shudder, her body spasming as she climaxed helplessly against his hand. The orgasm was powerful, rolling over her in waves that slowly, sweetly ebbed as she lay there, floating in an airy cocoon of momentary bliss.

It was abruptly shattered by an explosion of pain that cracked in the air, literally taking Julianna's breath away. Anders had smacked her spread and swollen pussy with a hard palm, the sting wiping away all the pleasure in a blinding instant. Julianna screamed, slamming her legs together against the unexpected sharp sting.

Anders leaned over and kissed her cheek. "Just as in life, so it is here, Julianna. With the pleasure comes the pain."

She lay there in shock, a slow fury moving through her. She was as angry at herself as she was at him. Stupid girl, to allow herself to be lulled by his seeming kindness and gentle attention. He was a trainer in a fucking slave camp. How had she been so stupid as to lower her guard, even for an instant? She silently promised herself she would do better.

Thankfully, he rose from the bed, moving away from her. She didn't even turn to see what he was doing. She lay still and quiet, curling herself into a fetal position on the soft quilt, wishing he would disappear. She drifted in a semi-daze for a while, just glad to be left alone.

She must have fallen asleep, because she found herself being pulled from a dream by the sound of Anders' voice. "Wake up." She sat up, instantly wide awake and wondering with trepidation what was next.

"Do you need to pee?" Anders asked.

Her bladder awoke at the question. "Yes…sir."

He nodded but said nothing more. She looked around the room, seeing and then looking away from the image of herself reflected in the mirrored wall, huddled small and pale on the bed, her hair wild around her face. She didn't see a toilet. Perhaps he was going to lead her to it. She swung her feet over the side of the bed, ready to follow, eager to relieve herself.

"I didn't tell you to get up, did I?" He raised a brow.

"Uh, no, but you said—"

He cut her off. "I asked you a question, that is all."

"But I thought—"

"Hush now. You are being disobedient. A slave does not speak unless asked a direct question, or granted permission, neither of which has taken place here."

"But..." Julianna trailed off, frightened, confused and angry as she stared at the handsome man. He was tall, easily several inches over six feet. He was wearing a white T-shirt that showed off the bulges of his biceps and the straight line of his broad shoulders. His jeans shorts showed his tan muscular legs, covered in downy golden blond hair. How could someone so good looking be doing what he was doing?

She knew that was a dumb question—goodness or evil had nothing to do with how one looked. Or acted, for that matter. The tenderness and gentleness he'd displayed their first hour together had been shattered with the stinging blow of his palm. She wouldn't be fooled again. She would be on her guard.

He went to the sink and returned a moment later with a glass of water. "Drink."

"But I—"

"I didn't ask you to speak."

Julianna clamped her mouth shut and took the offered glass. She drank, aware she was hungry again. "All of it," he commanded, when she stopped halfway. Julianna forced herself to finish the glass. After all, who knew when she might get more? When she was done, he took it from her and set it aside.

"Would you like to pee now?"

"Yes, sir."

"It's good to want things." *Bastard,* she thought. She watched tensely as he picked up a low stool from a corner and placed it in front of the mirrored wall. "Come sit down here, facing the mirror." When she didn't move right away, he added, "Go on, do as you're told."

Reluctantly, Julianna got up and moved toward the mirrored wall. She sat on the low stool, knees pressed together. Anders joined her, settling himself in a cross-legged position beside her on the floor. "Scoot back a little and spread your knees wide open. Put your hands behind your head, elbows out."

Julianna obeyed, closing her eyes. "Look at yourself," he said. "Open your eyes and look in the mirror." Julianna looked, embarrassed to see her shaven pussy exposed like this. She let her eyes go out of focus, reducing the image to a blur.

Even so she could feel his eyes in the mirror, moving over her nakedness as if he had every right to do so. She wanted to scream. She wanted to claw his beautiful blue eyes out to keep him from staring at her. She wanted to kill him. Instead she kept her fingers laced behind her neck and did nothing. Nothing at all. What choice did she have?

Anders reached for her sex, stroking her labia, his touch as light as before. He rubbed over her clit and then licked his finger before sliding it inside her. She felt her vaginal muscles clamping involuntarily against him. She felt the pressure against her bladder. He withdrew the finger and, adding a second, moved them over her labia, rubbing directly on her clit until she let out a breath and her eyes fluttered shut.

"Eyes open," Anders snapped. Then, more gently, "I want you to focus now." He dropped his hand. "Whatever I do to you," he continued, "you are to maintain your position on the stool, knees wide apart. If you close your legs or lower your arms, we'll just have to start again. Do you understand?"

"Yes, sir." Julianna's heart had begun to race in fearful expectation and dread. What was he going to do to her?

"I want you to watch in the mirror. Keep your eyes open and watch." He crouched just behind her, reaching his arm over her body, his hand now obscuring her sex from view. With a rapid movement, he smacked her pussy, the sound cracking the air.

"Ow!" Julianna jerked and automatically slammed her knees shut.

"Naughty girl," Anders said calmly. "You're already out of position. We will start over." He waited while she forced herself to spread her knees again. "Keep your eyes open," he said, and again he smacked her. She was more prepared and managed to hold her legs apart. It hurt, but it wasn't intolerable.

He struck her again, several hard, rapid blows, followed by more gentle smacks, almost strokes, catching her clit with his fingers as they moved upward, mixing the pleasure and the pain. She could feel her clit engorging from the stroking of his hand and then all at once the stroking was replaced by the sharp, painful sting of his palm. She yelped, again shutting her legs.

"And we start again," he said calmly, staring her down with those vivid blue eyes until she spread her legs. "Wider." She obeyed.

This time he struck her very hard, nearly knocking her sideways from the stool with the blow. Yelping with pain, instinctively she reached out to break her fall. He shook his head, the thick blond hair swaying over his forehead. "Back in position. Spread your legs."

Julianna's pussy was throbbing from the sting, the skin tender and sore. She looked at her tormentor with pleading eyes. "I can't—"

"You can do anything I tell you to do. I will teach you discipline. Now spread your legs."

With a tremulous sigh, Julianna obeyed. She managed to maintain her position as he smacked her poor pussy hard, over and over until the sting began to numb into something bearable.

I can do this, she told herself, grimacing at her reflection. *I can get through this. It won't go on forever. Maybe then he'll let me pee.*

Slowly he eased the smacking until he was again rubbing and brushing his fingers against her now swollen, aching sex in a sensual, steady stroke that, despite herself, soon had her panting as she tried to resist the rising pleasure moving through her loins.

I won't come again. I won't, she vowed, certain if she did, she would pay for it one way or the other. But, oh, it felt so good, his skillful, tender touch easing away the sting. *No. Don't come. Don't give the bastard the satisfaction of knowing he can do that to you.* She drew in a breath, refusing to succumb to his sensual touch. He was leaning over her, his broad chest against her back, his second hand now cupping her breast, rolling the nipple between his fingers.

In spite of her promise to herself, she could feel the bud of an orgasm threatening to bloom. As if sensing this, Anders pressed two fingers inside her, crooking them as he had before and again finding that sensitive spot.

She was breathing hard and her fingers slipped apart, her hands falling limply to her sides as her head fell back against Anders' shoulder. "Oh god," she breathed. He dropped his second hand from her breast, using the tips of his fingers to roll her clit while the fingers inside her wrought their strange magic. She gave up. Why fight when he was going to win, no matter what? She let go, waves of orgasmic pleasure rushing through her body.

Anders pushed her thighs wide apart; they must have fallen closed during her climax. Before she could react, he struck her inner thighs hard with his open hands, leaving the imprint on her skin. As she gasped from the unexpected blows, he smacked her spread pussy, five times in rapid, painful succession.

He stood and she fell forward from the stool, resting her forehead against the cool glass of the mirror, clasping her stinging sex in both hands. She became aware of him standing beside her. He was wearing sandals and even his feet were beautiful, the toes long and straight, the nails perfectly groomed. It was an odd thing to notice, but since she'd been forced to spend so much time on her knees, ordered to kiss the feet of her captors, she supposed it made sense.

She suddenly realized that's what he must be waiting for. Best to get it over with. Julianna scooted closer, touching her lips to the top of one of Ander's feet. "Thank you, sir," she mumbled, "for using this worthless slave."

She felt his hands on her shoulders. He gripped her arms and pulled her upright, turning her so she was facing him. He held her against his chest and whispered in her ear. "You are not worthless. And once trained, you will be worth your weight in gold."

Julianna's bladder ached from the pressure. She could barely pay attention to what Anders was saying. She crossed her legs, afraid she might end up wetting herself before she made it to the toilet. He let her go and she stepped back, wondering where the bathroom was. Reading her mind, Anders pointed to a bucket beneath the freestanding sink.

She looked from the bucket to him and back at the bucket. "Modesty," he informed her, "has no place for you now. Bring the bucket to me."

Julianna dragged the plastic bucket, which smelled of stale urine and bleach, and set it in front of him as ordered. Anders stood with his hands on his hips. "Now straddle it, put your hands behind your head and keep your eyes on my face while you pee."

Placing a leg on either side, she squatted, trying to balance as she laced her fingers behind her head. For a long, painful moment, her body refused to obey her need. She stared into the handsome man's face as ordered, recalling his remark about the anger he had seen on her face.

She wouldn't let him see that anger again. For some reason the lyrics to an old song came into her mind: *And when they stare, just let them burn their eyes.* Holding her head high, she willed her face into calm repose, or at least she hoped she was managing to do that, despite the impotent rage seething inside her.

The urine released, haltingly at first, then in a steady, hot stream into the bucket. When she was done, Julianna didn't ask for toilet paper. She didn't say a word. Still squatting and in position, she kept her eyes on his face and waited.

He let her stay that way for perhaps thirty seconds his eyes moving over her face and body. She didn't move a muscle or make a sound. When he finally moved to the sink, she felt as if she'd achieved a small victory of sorts.

He returned with toilet paper, which he used on her and then dropped into the bucket. "Place the bucket in the hall, just outside the door," he ordered. "It's time for your next task."

Chapter 6

As Julianna set the bucket outside the door, it occurred to her she could make a run for it. She could race down the hallway and fly out the door. If she managed to make it that far, then what? Could she make it to the dock? Could she get into the boat, somehow get it unmoored and the engine started? Or maybe she could hide out among the palm trees, waiting till dark to try and make her escape.

Even as these thoughts whizzed through her brain, she saw the man she had dubbed Fox leaning casually against the wall outside the door. He looked at her, a small smile moving over his face. Julianna left the bucket and ducked back into the room, daunted but not, she told herself firmly, defeated.

The bucket must have been a signal, because as soon as she was back in the room, there was a knock and Fox opened the door. He was holding a large coil of rope in one hand, a pair of scissors in the other.

"Have you ever been bound as part of sexual play, Julianna?" Anders asked. Julianna stared at him. "A direct question," he prompted softly.

"No, sir," she replied, nervously eyeing the rope.

"Pete, you know what to do." *Pete.* Fox suited him better, Julianna thought, as she mentally adjusted to his real name. As he moved toward her, Julianna shrank back, but there was nowhere to go. "Hands behind your back," Anders instructed. Pete moved behind her, winding the rope around her upper arms, forcing her to arch to accommodate the tension of her bindings. He wound the rope around her wrists and then pulled it up between her legs, tugging it up uncomfortably between her pussy lips and wrapping it around her waist.

While Pete was working, Anders said, "There is a certain freedom in bondage, as ironic as that might sound to you. But think about it. You don't have to hold your position—it's held for you. You won't be taking your arms from behind your back by accident because you can't. You won't forget your posture, breasts thrust proudly forward, because you have no choice in the matter." He reached for her face and for a second she thought he was going to slap her, but he caressed her cheek, tucking a tendril of hair behind her ear.

"Freedom is an illusion, Julianna," he murmured close to her ear. "It always comes with a price." Stepping back, he pressed her shoulder. "Kneel. It's time for your next lesson."

She lowered herself awkwardly to the floor, nearly losing her balance in the process. The binds were tight and her arms were tingling. She flexed her fingers and pulled against the ropes but she was well and truly bound. Pete was behind her, tying her ankles together. One push, she realized, would send her falling to her side with no way to break her fall.

"Are you hungry?" Anders asked.

"Yes, sir."

Anders nodded toward Pete, who left the room, returning a few moments later with a tray. On the tray was a bowl of water and a plate with chunks of yellow cheese, bright red strawberries and what looked like peanut butter spread on small round crackers. Julianna's stomach gurgled and she stared longingly at the food.

Anders retrieved the low stool he'd had her sit on before. He sat down beside her as Pete moved in front of her. At a nod from Anders, to Julianna's shocked dismay, Pete opened his pants and slid them, along with his underwear, to his knees. He moved closer to her, his penis dangling before her, nestled in a profusion of auburn pubic hair. She could smell his sweat and musk.

Julianna turned her head away, closing her eyes. She wanted to cry with frustration. She wanted to scream that she'd rather starve than suck this man's cock. She said nothing, the food whispering to her to be silent.

"Time to test your skills," Anders said. "Every good slave must properly worship her Master. Your task today is made more difficult since you are deprived of the use of your hands. To make matters more challenging, Pete is gay. You'll have to use every bit of your skill and attention to not only get him hard, but make him come."

Julianna felt as if she were pinned to the spot; frozen in place. She would not—she could not—put her mouth on that man's cock. Anders reached toward her and grabbed a handful of her hair, pulling back hard and forcing her face toward the ceiling. Leaning close, he spoke in a soft, gentle voice totally incongruous with his actions. "Please me, Julianna. You have done so well this far. Don't disappoint me now."

He let go of her hair and sat back on the stool. Julianna swallowed and blinked away the tears the hair pulling had caused. She leaned forward, trying not to inhale as she hesitantly touched her tongue to the long but still soft shaft. Tentatively she sucked it into her mouth and glided her tongue in a circle around the head. Nothing seemed to be happening. She let the limp shaft fall from her lips and glanced helplessly at Anders.

"Try licking his balls," he offered. "Pete likes that." Julianna turned back to her task, the prospect of licking this man's hairy balls not at all appealing. The thought of the food waiting for her spurred her to action. She leaned forward again, licking at the hairy sac and then taking the balls gently into her mouth. Pete groaned his approval.

She could feel the shaft begin to harden against her cheek as she tongued his balls. Leaning back, she maneuvered until she captured the head of his growing cock between her lips. As she sucked at it, the shaft continued to fatten and elongate. She closed her eyes, trying to recall the face of a man in her past who had attracted her. She couldn't think of anyone, anyone at all. The only face that rose in her mind's eye was that of Anders', with its Nordic perfection. Still that was better than pointy-faced Fox and so she allowed the image to remain.

She bobbed up and down along the now-erect shaft. It was bigger than any cock she'd ever seen, not that she'd seen that many, and she was having a very hard time getting much of it into her mouth. If only she'd had the use of her hands, she would have a much better chance of getting this gay man to come.

Not knowing what else to do, she focused on the sensitive gland just below the head, flicking it with her tongue, wondering how long this was going to take, as her jaw had begun to ache and her arms were falling asleep behind her back.

"I don't feel your enthusiasm," Anders remarked drily.

That's because I don't have any, you dumb fuck. Not that she could have voiced this thought even if she was stupid enough to try, with the head of Pete's thick cock in her mouth.

All at once she felt a hand on the back of her head as Anders pressed her forward, forcing her to take more and more of the cock into her mouth. As the head of it poked into her throat, Julianna began to gag and reflexively pushed back against Anders' hand.

"Open your throat. Stop fighting." Anders kept his hand firmly on the back of Julianna's head. She sputtered and choked against the huge member, panic rising in her gut as she struggled to breathe. "Let go," Anders urged, stroking her hair, though still keeping her impaled on the shaft. "When I feel you surrender, I'll let you breathe. Let go, Julianna. Open yourself to him."

Somehow she managed to relax her throat muscles enough to ease the spasm of her gagging. The head slipped farther back in her throat, completely blocking her windpipe, but at that moment Anders let go and she reared back, gasping for air. The cock fell from her mouth, bobbing lewdly toward her, the fat head nearly purple.

"We have a lot of work to do," Anders said. "Cock worship will be high on your list of skills to learn. Now go on." He touched the back of her head. "Make this worthy gentleman come. I know you can do it."

Julianna's eye fell on the food waiting on tray. Closing her eyes she leaned forward again, taking the head of the shaft back into her mouth.

She focused on relaxing her throat, trying to fool herself into pretending this was her lover. She hated the way he smelled and tasted. She hated everything about this man and this setup. No, she just wasn't up to that level of self-deception, so she tried to focus on doing the best she could in order to get it over with as soon as possible.

She licked her way along the shaft and then sucked him in as deep as she could, massaging the length of him with her lips, tongue and throat. She moved her mouth up and down, trying to create friction with her lips to give him whatever stimulation it was he needed to get off. It was possible he *couldn't* come with a woman, but Julianna knew she had to keep trying.

Finally, to her great relief, Pete began to grunt. He thrust forward, reaching for her shoulders to hold her in place while he groaned and shot globs of ejaculate down her throat. He had thrust so far back as he was coming that she couldn't even swallow, which was probably a good thing, as she doubted she would have been able to force it down without vomiting.

He let go of her shoulders and stepped back. "Lick him clean," Anders said softly, "and then kiss his feet and thank him properly. Then you shall have your meal."

The promise of food cut off the protest rising of its own accord in her throat. The worst was over—she had finished the task. She could do this last bit of nonsense. Strawberries and cheese awaited her. She licked a lingering drop of cum from the tip of the shrinking shaft.

"You can do better than that," Anders said. With a barely suppressed sigh, Julianna forced her lips over the head of his cock. Pete obliged her, if it could be called obliging, by gripping the base of his shaft and yanking upwards, which had the result of producing a salty, gooey deposit of the last of his cum onto her tongue.

Trying to keep from gagging, Julianna lowered herself carefully so as not to fall over, uncomfortably bound as she was. She brushed her lips over the top of each dusty black boot. "Thank you, sir," she said, forcing the words out, "for using this worthless slave."

Pete pulled up his pants and tucked his privates away. At a nod from Anders he moved behind Julianna and unknotted and unwound the ropes that bound her. Her arms fell heavily to her sides, numb from tight bonds. Anders picked up the tray and placed it on the floor beside the bed.

Once her ankles were free, Pete took the rope and left the room. Anders bent beside Julianna and lifted her into his arms. He settled on the edge of the bed with her in his lap. He massaged her arms, one after the other as they tingled painfully back to life.

"You get an A for effort. Pete is difficult to arouse when it's a woman at his feet. As to skill, well..." He shrugged. "I'd say a C minus. But that's all right. By the time I'm done with you, you'll have the skills you need to properly worship a man's cock. Not only the skill, but the grace." He put one arm around her waist to hold her steady on his lap.

"You must learn to serve with grace and enthusiasm, no matter the task. You exist to serve, Julianna. That is your life now." He reached for the plate of food and picked up a cracker slathered in peanut butter and held it near her mouth. "I shall feed you."

Eagerly she leaned toward the cracker, mouth open. He placed it on her tongue. The peanut butter was rich and creamy, a perfect complement to the salty, crunchy cracker that held it. She tried to chew slowly and savor its perfection. Then she saw the plump strawberry he held between his fingers and she swallowed quickly, ready to receive the succulent fruit. He gave her cheese and more fruit, and then tilted the bowl of water to her lips.

Some of it spilled over her breasts as she drank but she barely noticed, lost in the pleasure of food and drink, and the comfort of being held. He fed her until every morsel was gone from the plate. His fingers were stained with strawberry juice and as he held them close to her mouth, she licked them. "Greedy girl," he said, but he was smiling.

He stood, lifting her in the process and setting her down on her feet. "You've done well today. Time for you to rest. You'll have a full day ahead of you tomorrow." Julianna eyed the bed, quite ready to climb beneath that soft quilt and snuggle against the pillows.

Anders saw where she was looking and shook his head. "This room is for training purposes. But don't worry. You'll be back."

Pete knocked lightly and reentered the room, his face impassive as if he hadn't just had his cock down her throat. He waited while Anders retrieved something from a shelf and moved to Julianna. "This is your collar," Anders said. "You will wear it for the duration of your stay here."

The collar was like those she'd seen on the girls sleeping in their cells when she'd been led down the hall. It was wide but thankfully not as stiff as it looked. There were large, sturdy O-rings on the sides, back and front of the collar. Anders placed it around her neck and slipped a small padlock over the buckle at the back, removing and pocketing the key. He kissed the top of her head and stepped back as Pete led her out of the room and down the hallway.

Pete opened the door of an empty cell, guiding Julianna inside. He reached for the long chain that was lying beneath her bed and attached it to the ring at the front of her collar. The chain was long enough to allow her to move around the small cell. Without a word, he turned and walked out, shutting the barred door with a clang and turning the bolt that locked her in. As he moved away down the hall, Julianna thought about what a strange life he'd chosen for himself.

The fluorescent light in the ceiling of Julianna's cell suddenly flickered out. The entire building was plunged into darkness. Feeling her way, Julianna climbed onto the thin mattress, a far cry from the luxury bed in Ander's training room.

When she tugged at the thick collar around her neck, it caused the chain to clink along the stone floor. There was no blanket, not even a sheet to pull up around her. So she curled into a tight fetal ball on her side. She lay there for a long time, thinking about her life before the abduction, and how much she had taken for granted.

She was only twenty-three—at the beginning of her life. Did it really end here, as they terrorized and brainwashed her into submission and slavery? "No," she said aloud. "No. I won't let it happen. It's just not an option." Somehow, some way, she would *not* let it end here. She would find a way to escape, and once she was free, she would live her life as if each day were her last.

As she drifted into a dream, the bars of the cell melted around her and the collar vanished from her neck. She was a little girl again, and she'd just awoken from a nightmare. She padded down the hall to her mother's bedroom and climbed into the bed piled with old patchwork quilts beside her sleeping mother.

"I had a bad dream, Mama, can I sleep with you?"

Mama rolled over and opened her arms. "Sure, baby." As she held Julianna close, Mama kissed her forehead. "There," she said. "That kiss is magic, you know. It will protect you all night long from any more bad dreams."

"Thank you, Mama," Julianna whispered, as she snuggled against her mother's warm, soft body and closed her eyes, falling into a deep, dreamless sleep.

~*~

The Spaniard brought her breakfast. He left a cart outside the door, like the ones used in hospitals to bring around the meals. How many women were incarcerated here, she wondered? How long until she was moved out for sale? The thought was too frightening to contemplate, and she pushed it from her mind.

He set her tray on the floor and pointed to the ground. Julianna scrambled from the cot and knelt before the food. At least she was getting regular meals now. To her annoyance, he cuffed her hands behind her back but at least she was left alone to eat, and she was grateful for this small relief. She was just finishing the sausage patties and eggs when he returned, a leash in his hand.

"Let's go." Leaning down, he clipped the leash to her collar and jerked it gently. She rose and followed the guard out of the cell. Pete was just ahead of them, pulling another woman along in his wake. She, like Julianna, was naked, her ass mottled with purple bruises.

The Spaniard led Julianna into the showers. The other girl was standing by the wall, arms out, eyes downcast. She was shaven too, her breasts high and small, her ribs delicately etched on a too-thin body. Her hair was short and very blond. She barely looked out of her teens, if that. What family had she left behind? Julianna's heart ached for the girl's parents and for that one moment, she was glad she was an orphan.

The girl didn't even look up when Julianna was led to stand beside her. The Spaniard released her cuffs from behind her back and removed them. She expected him to re-cuff and secure her to the wall like the last time, but instead he shoved them into his pocket. He produced a small key from a chain around his neck. The collars of both girls were unlocked and removed, and Julianna reached up to massage her neck. The other girl didn't move a muscle.

While the guards were putting on their rubber aprons, Julianna whispered, "Hey," but the girl didn't respond in any way. She might have been a mannequin or a robot, Julianna thought, horrified. Was this going to happen to her?

"Arms out," Pete said. "Legs spread." The girl beside Julianna obeyed as if she was in a trance, but at least it showed she could hear and process things. The men approached and turned on the hoses. As the cold spray hit them, Julianna tried to make eye contact with the girl, but she never looked up from the ground.

The girl was done first and was led to the shaving table by the Spaniard, while Pete washed Julianna's hair.

When it was Julianna's turn on the shaving table, the girl waited, kneeling and silent beside them, her eyes on the floor.

Collars and cuffs were replaced and leashes attached, and the girls were led out of the shower room. Julianna had expected they would be led either back to their respective cells or to different rooms, but they were both pulled along to what Julianna recognized as Stephen's torture chamber.

Julianna's muscles tensed, her fight or flight reflexes kicking in. Adrenaline was zipping through her bloodstream. Was she just going to walk passively along beside this girl, letting these two strange, silent men lead them to the next horror? How many women were on this island? What if they were to band together, to rise up and somehow take back control of their lives? She had seen no guns, no weapons other than sheer brute force.

She knew even as these thoughts flickered in her brain that it was useless. The girl beside her appeared to be little more than a zombie, resigned to her fate, perhaps even so damaged by what she'd been through that she'd literally lost her mind. No, if Julianna was going to make a break, she'd have to do it on her own. For the moment she could do nothing but pretend to go along with the insanity of this place. She didn't dare resist, not yet. She would pay too high a price for no gain. But somehow, she promised herself, she would get out of this. She had to. She would not allow herself to end up like the poor girl walking so meekly beside her.

Chapter 7

As they entered the room Julianna saw that the medical exam table had been pushed against the wall. There were two mats placed side-by-side on the floor. They were led to these and jerked downward. The girl immediately moved into a kneeling up at-attention pose and Julianna followed suit. Their elbows nearly touched.

The guards walked out, leaving the two girls alone. As Julianna followed their exit with her gaze, she noticed a tall, narrow cage with thin black bars set against the wall. She hadn't remembered seeing that before. There were metal cuffs at the corners, both top and bottom. Who, she wondered, would be going in there?

She glanced sidelong at the girl. "My name is Julianna," she whispered. The girl was still as stone—not even a flicker of animation moved over her face. "What's your name?" Julianna tried again, barely moving her lips just in case they were being observed. Still nothing.

All right, then, Julianna thought, *I'll call you Sandy.*

The door opened and Stephen appeared, coming into the room and stopping in front of them, a single tail whip in his hand. "Good morning. How are you today, number thirty-one?" He looked at the blond girl with what seemed like actual fondness.

Sandy lifted her head, her eyes wide, a soft, shy smile playing on her rosebud lips. She seemed to radiate a kind of submissive innocence that belied the robot-like demeanor she'd exhibited a moment before. When she spoke, her voice was low and respectful.

"I'm very well, sir. Thank you for asking."

Julianna turned to stare at the suddenly transformed girl beside her. Stephen reached down, roughly cuffing her on the side of the head. "Eyes straight ahead, thirty-eight. You're here this morning to observe and learn something. Number thirty-one is very close to being sale-worthy. She can focus and knows how to please a man. She has not only accepted, but embraced her fate, isn't that right, thirty-one?"

"Yes, sir. Thank you, sir." Sandy ducked her head in an almost-coquettish way, her small mouth lifting at the corners. The change in her demeanor and behavior was striking now that the trainer was in the room. Apparently the girl didn't feel the need to put on that particular show for the guards. A thought suddenly slipped its way into Julianna's mind—were the guards themselves there of their own free will? What kind of ties kept them on the island? Was it really all about the money?

Her train of thought was disturbed by the Spaniard and Pete as they reentered the room. They had removed their black pants and tops, and were now wearing nothing but red thongs. Both men had hard, muscular bodies. The Spaniard, Julianna noted, had pierced nipples.

Stephen looked up as they entered. "Put number thirty-eight in the cage. Secure and gag her." Before Julianna could react, the two men were on her, hauling her up and dragging her toward the cage. Pete pushed her inside while the Spaniard knelt and secured her ankles into the waiting cuffs. Pete forced her wrists into the upper cuffs, stretching her like an X. Stephen handed Pete a large red ball gag, which he forced between Julianna's lips and then reached over her head to buckle in place. Using a large metal clip, he attached the O-ring on her collar to one of the bars of the cage.

While this was going on, Sandy remained kneeling up with her hands behind her head, her back arched, her eyes fixed with what looked like adoration on Stephen. Stephen stroked the girl's breasts and pulled at her small nipples in an absent way while he watched Julianna being chained and gagged.

The rubber ball gag was fat and tasted strongly of rubber. It forced her tongue back uncomfortably as she tried to maneuver it into a more tolerable position. With the collar and cuffs holding her in place, her body was forced flush against the hard, narrow bars of the cage.

Both guards returned to stand in front of Sandy, giving Julianna a profile view of the three of them. The men had their hands behind their backs, their groins level with Sandy's face. Something in the way they stood again gave Julianna the sense they were more, or rather less, than mere guards on the island.

Stephen stood just behind Sandy, the long, cruel whip in his hands. He looked toward Julianna. "Pay attention, thirty-eight. This is what you are striving for. See how a real slave behaves."

He stroked Sandy's head. "You know what to do." For a split second, Sandy's eyes veered toward Julianna in the cage. It happened so quickly, Julianna decided she must have imagined it, but she could have sworn she'd seen fire in that gaze, a most decidedly un-submissive fire.

Sandy leaned toward Pete first, hooking her fingers beneath the elastic of his thong and dragging it down his legs, revealing the long, thick shaft Julianna had been forced to suck the day before. Next she leaned toward the Spaniard, repeating the action. She sucked his cock into her mouth first, while cupping his balls in her small hands. She bobbed there until the shaft was fully erect. Letting it go, she returned her focus to the other man, bringing him to erection as well.

She barely jerked when the tip of the single tail flicked at her ass with a popping sound. A small red mark appeared on her already bruised bottom. A flicker of pain moved over her features when the whip struck her back, but she didn't seem to miss a beat as she moved back and forth between the two men.

Stephen began to whip her steadily, the leather snapping against the girl's fair skin, leaving red marks with each cruel stroke until her back and ass were mottled, but she never made a sound. She appeared to be absorbed in her task, licking and teasing one man and then the other until at last the Spaniard groaned and reached for her head, keeping her in position while he thrust against her face, her nose pressed against his pubic bone.

"That's it. Take Jorge's offering. This is why you exist." Stephen continued to whip her. When the Spaniard—or rather, Jorge—finally let her go, Sandy swallowed and licked her lips, catching a trickle of semen at the corner of her mouth with her tongue. She knelt and kissed Jorge's foot. "Thank you, sir, for allowing this worthless slave to worship your cock." Her low, sultry voice didn't seem to fit with the slip of a girl she was.

"Oh!" A particularly savage cut of the whip made her eyes widen and tears spilled over. Julianna's heart ached for the girl and she found she was clenching the bars of the cage in impotent fury over the scene she was being forced to watch.

"Focus," Stephen intoned.

Sandy drew in a deep, shuddering breath, her utter composure damaged by his cruel blow. As she leaned toward Pete, the whip wrapped suddenly around her narrow torso, leaving an angry red mark on her breast. Sandy gasped and Julianna could see the pain rippling over her face. She blew out a breath and managed to take Pete's cock into her mouth.

Wrapping a hand around the base of the long shaft, she reached back to press her fingers between his ass cheeks. Pete responded with a guttural moan and thrust against her. He came much more quickly with Sandy than he had for Julianna. Clearly this wasn't the first time Sandy had been through this exercise with the guards.

"Thank you, sir, for allowing this worthless slave to please you," Sandy purred, as she kissed his foot. Then she straightened up, lacing her fingers behind her head as Stephen continued flicking his wrist, catching her with the tip of the biting lash.

Sandy's eyes were closed, tears coursing down her cheeks, yet she barely flinched with each flick of the whip. The guards hadn't moved—their underwear still at their ankles, their cocks dangling, hands again behind their backs. Julianna looked at Stephen and was horrified by the expression on his face.

His eyes were wide, a wild fire glowing behind them. His lips were parted, the tip of his tongue showing as he continued to beat the hapless girl kneeling before him. His erection bulged beneath the thin khaki slacks he wore. All at once he dropped the whip and jerked Sandy's shoulder, pulling her around to face him. Tearing open his pants, he shoved his cock down her throat with one brutal gesture, gagging her as he moved roughly in and out of her mouth, his hands on either side of her head holding her in position.

He didn't groan or grunt as the guards had, but lifted his chin, his eyes closed, the tendons in his neck straining as he pummeled the girl without mercy. Finally he let her go, pushing her back so that she fell with a soft cry as she hit the mat. Julianna realized tears were tracking down her own face and she bit down hard on the ball gag, murderous rage in her heart.

Sandy scrambled back to her knees and knelt at Stephen's feet, kissing the tops of his sandals and thanking him, her voice finally cracking from the ordeal. Stephen zipped up his pants and stood impassively, the fire gone from his eyes, which were cold and hard once more.

He placed a hand on the top of Sandy's head, patting her as if she were his dog. He turned his gaze to Julianna. "Let her out, boys." The guards pulled their thongs back into place and approached the cage. As they were busy opening the cuffs, Stephen turned away, replacing the whip in a rack in the corner of the room.

Sandy was again kneeling up in an at-attention position, her eyes on the floor. Who would "buy" this girl? She looked so delicate, so small, and with her shaven pubis, more like a child than a woman. Had someone already chosen her from the photo gallery and paid his cold, hard cash to possess her? Poor Sandy, broken down and rebuilt into this a brainwashed slave girl, trained to perform on command and then parrot her thanks for being abused. Could this happen to Julianna as well? Would she, as Stephen insisted, succumb as they all did, despite her determination to resist?

The guards pulled her from the cage. Pete unbuckled the gag and Julianna struggled to swallow the saliva that had pooled in her mouth. Stephen waved his hand imperiously at the guards. "You may go."

As they filed out, he turned to Sandy. "You've earned a reward, thirty-one." He pointed to the mat. "I think we'll combine thirty-eight's lesson with your reward. She's going to give you an orgasm. But remember, don't come until I say so."

"Yes, sir, thank you, sir." Sandy lay down on the mat, letting her legs fall open to reveal her shaven sex. Julianna felt hot embarrassment, both for herself and for the girl. She looked away.

"Get on your knees, thirty-eight. You ever licked pussy before?"

Julianna shook her head as she very reluctantly knelt in front of the girl. "Direct question!" Stephen barked.

"No, sir. I never have." *And I don't want to start now.* She knew she had no choice. If she were honest, she'd rather lick this poor, defenseless girl than touch the cock of any man on this godforsaken island. Still, she found herself very nervous at the prospect.

"Well, it isn't rocket science. I'm sure you can figure out what to do. Your job is to make her come. You will do your very best, not stopping until I say so. Even if she asks to come, and I forbid it, you are not to stop what you are doing, do you understand?"

Oh, yeah, I understand, you motherfucker. Just like you did to me. Make it impossible to resist, and then punish the person for coming. Now you want to use me to do the same to her. God, I hate you. Aloud she said, "Yes, sir."

"If you stop," he continued, "you'll be punished. By the same token, if you fail to make her come, you'll be punished as well. Do I make myself clear?"

As mud, you asshole. "Yes, sir."

Stephen pulled a higher stool over and sat down, crossing his arms over his chest. Julianna took a breath and pulled her hair back from her face, looping it into a ponytail. She knelt over Sandy, feeling embarrassed and unsure. Hesitantly she placed a hand on either slender thigh. She noticed a fine latticework of fading welts, though the skin felt soft beneath her fingers.

Sandy's labia were larger than her own, dark pink tinged with purple, the clit hidden beneath its hood. She had never looked at another woman's pussy like this, much less been so close to one. She wondered if Sandy were as nervous as she. She was lying still as a statue, her eyes closed, her hands at her sides, her feet flat on the floor, drawn up knees spread wide.

Julianna leaned tentatively forward, snaking out the tip of her tongue, which made contact with the soft folds of Sandy's smooth labia. She licked along the outer edges, aware she'd have to do better than this if she was going to make the girl come. She closed her eyes and shifted her focus to the inner labia, licking along the delicate curves. It wasn't so terrible. Maybe she could even give this poor girl some pleasure in the midst of the horror of their shared plight.

She moved her tongue in a slow, light circle, delicately teasing at the hidden clit with a careful flick of her tongue. Sandy moved slightly beneath her touch and let out the smallest of sighs.

Encouraged by this, Julianna continued to flick and lick at the hood until she felt the clit beneath begin to harden and swell. Recalling her own dislike of too much direct attention to the clit too early on, she eased off, licking in slow, easy swirls over the spicy-sweet flesh.

Sandy groaned, arching up toward Julianna. She couldn't deny the thrill it caused her to realize she was giving this woman at least some modicum of pleasure. She gripped tighter on Sandy's thighs and began to lap at her pussy with something approaching enthusiasm. Her tongue moved in circles, teasing around the clit and then licking it directly with slow, sweet intensity until Sandy groaned again, her hands coming up to cradle Julianna's head.

"Don't come, thirty-one. Not until I say so." Julianna had almost forgotten about the trainer and his voice, right by her head, made her jump. She became acutely self-conscious at the realization he was so close to them. Somehow she'd managed to block him out for those few short minutes when he'd left them alone. Now she stumbled a little, losing her rhythm. Sandy's hands fell away and Julianna realized her jaw was getting tired.

She closed her eyes and told herself to focus. *Block out the asshole. He doesn't exist. You're doing this for Sandy.* She started over, again licking along the outer labia, moving slowly in concentric circles toward her clit until Sandy was again moaning softly, arching her raised pelvis toward Julianna's tongue.

She grabbed Julianna's head again, forcing Julianna's nose against the girl's soft, smooth pubic mound as she continued to tongue her. Julianna was surprised at herself, at the complete lack of revulsion she had thought she would experience. The experience might even have been sexy, if the circumstances surrounding it weren't so odious. She liked the feel of the hard nubbin beneath its hood, which she tickled and teased with what skill she possessed. Sandy began to mewl, her fingers tightening in Julianna's hair.

"Don't stop," Stephen ordered, placing his hand on the back of Julianna's head. "And you, thirty-one, don't come."

"No, sir!" Sandy panted. Julianna could feel her trembling. She kept her mouth over the girl's sex, but stopped licking at her clit, though she continued to move her head in such a way that suggested she was. Sandy continued to writhe and moan beneath her. *Fuck you, dickhead Stephen,* she thought, pleased to be complicit with Sandy in their deception.

After a few minutes, Stephen took his hand away and sat back. "Okay, now. Do it, thirty-one. Come for me."

Julianna resumed her licking, lightly suckling the little marble beneath its silky hood until Sandy began to buck in earnest, her mewling cries escalating into gasps and moans as she shuddered and jerked beneath Julianna's kiss. Julianna held her thighs open as she licked her, determined not to stop until she was sure Sandy had milked all the possible pleasure from the experience.

It was Stephen who stopped her, pulling her back by the hair. Sandy rolled from the low stool and knelt in a servile crouch at Stephen's feet. "Thank you, sir, for allowing this worthless slave to come." She kissed his foot with reverence.

Julianna sat back on her heels, wiping her mouth with the back of her hand. Stephen glared at her until she, too, knelt at his feet, mouthing words that meant less than nothing to her.

There was a beeping sound from Stephen's pocket. He backed away from the girls and pulled out a small walkie-talkie, turning away from them as he spoke quietly into it. Julianna looked at Sandy, who had remained kneeling beside her. As if she could feel Julianna's eyes on her, Sandy lifted her gaze and once again their eyes met. There Julianna saw intelligence and passion, and that same spark of fire she had seen before.

Sandy moved her lips, though she made no sound.

Stephen turned around, moving back toward them. As if a light had been flicked off, the fire left Sandy's eyes and her face smoothed into a doll's mask. Julianna looked down, hoping her face was as smooth and devoid of emotion as Sandy's was. She had read the words formed on the girl's lips, and she took them to heart, feeling a tiny shoot of hope poke through her misery like a pale blade of spring grass. She rolled the words in her mind, wrapping them around herself like a blanket and repeating them over and over to herself.

Never give up.

Chapter 8

Julianna was on Anders' bed, spread eagle with her wrists and ankles roped at the corners of the mattress, her hips raised by several pillows beneath her ass. Anders sat beside her, running his hands over her bare body. He had set a short, thin cane with a black leather handle on the bed beside her. She didn't want to think about how it might be used.

"You are beautiful, Julianna." Anders ran his fingers over her breasts and lightly squeezed her rising nipples. His other hand trailed down her stomach and paused over her pussy, the fingers moving with butterfly lightness.

As he touched her, he said, "Today you will begin to learn orgasm control. Your ultimate goal is to accept whatever pleasure is offered you, but never to climax until your Master gives his permission. On the flip side of that, you must learn to come on command, but that will be for a different day."

He lifted his hand from her pussy and touched his fingers to her mouth, pushing past her lips to wet them with her saliva. He placed the wet fingers on her spread sex, teasing in a circle around her clit and moving down to her entrance. Pressing gently inside her, he found that sensitive spot again. As he stroked and teased her, Julianna found herself moaning. She clamped her mouth shut, again angry at herself for responding so easily to this man.

He leaned over and kissed her cheek. "Don't fight your reactions. Let them flow. I love how responsive you are, Julianna. You will make your Master very happy one day."

If this was supposed to be a compliment, it had the opposite effect. Julianna wanted to scratch the man's eyes out. She tugged at the ropes that held her wrists, determined not to respond to his touch again.

His fingers moved relentlessly inside her while she struggled to ignore the sensations he was creating. Finally slipping them out, he drew them up along her labia and began to rub her clit in light, even strokes. His touch was at once gentle and insistent. Julianna closed her eyes and blew out a breath, trying to fight the rising pleasure, powerless to close her legs or resist him in any way.

"Ooh," she heard herself moaning, despite her promises.

"Ask permission."

No. She would not come. She wouldn't give him the satisfaction. She wasn't his object, goddamn it, no matter how skilled he might be with his fingers. She felt the impending orgasm recede and silently congratulated herself. *Fuck you, Anders,* she thought.

Perhaps he sensed her withdrawal, because he again pressed his fingers inside her. She was wet now with her own juices and the fingers glided in easily, moving sensually inside her, making her catch her breath as he found the sweet spot. She was breathing hard, almost a pant, despite her efforts to control herself.

His fingers still buried inside her, he used his other hand to tease her hard clit. "Fuck," she blurted breathlessly.

"Ask permission."

Oh god, she couldn't help it. She started to buck against his hands. All at once the hands were withdrawn and a sharp, slicing sting of the cane took their place. Julianna screamed, her orgasm abruptly curtailed by the pain.

Instinctively she tried desperately to close her legs, but she was completely immobilized by the ropes. He struck her again and again, a steady hard tapping against the sensitive swollen folds of her sex, though nothing like as hard as the first stroke. He was hitting her lightly, but in a constant, stinging barrage that made her jerk and yelp.

Then, as abruptly as he'd started, Anders dropped the cane, his fingers soothing away the sting. "Ask next time, won't you?" His tone was light, as if he was just asking nicely for a favor, while she whimpered, hating him.

Again he began the slow, sensual tease, using both hands, slowly increasing the pace and intensity until she again found herself teetering on the edge of an orgasm. "Ooh," she gasped, and then, the memory of the cane still sharp, "Can I come? Please, sir?"

"No."

It was too late. Her body had taken over and she felt herself tumbling into a powerful climax. At the height of it, pain sliced through her consciousness, ripping a scream from her throat, a single brutal stroke. Again he followed up with a series of light taps as she whimpered, trying vainly to twist away.

Finally he set down the cane and shifted so he was kneeling between her legs. "Dearest Julianna." He stroked the hair from her face. "Why did you make me do that? Did you not understand that it wasn't enough to merely ask for permission? It had to be granted as well." He shook his head, offering an indulgent smile. "Perhaps that was my fault. I didn't make myself clear. Let's try again, shall we?"

This was worse, in its own insidious way, than anything Stephen had done to her. At least he was straight up about what he was doing—torture, pure and simple. Anders hid his sadism in the guise of a caring lover. God, how she hated him. She wanted to spit in his face. She wanted to smash him against the wall.

He loomed over her, a thick swatch of straight golden blond hair falling over his forehead. He smiled. "A direct question. Answer me."

She didn't know what the question had been, barely able to concentrate on his babble through the din of her own rage. "I—I don't know what you asked...sir."

"Pay attention," he snapped, but then smiled again, slow and sensual. "I suggested that we try it again. I'm going to make you come, and you're going to ask permission. If you come before that permission is granted, you will be reminded," he lifted the cane and held it before her, "of your error. Does that suit you, Julianna?"

She stared at him. What did he expect her to say? The truth? That she'd rather drink acid than spend another second tied down on his soft bed, submitting to his cruel games? Or did she lie, pretending, as Sandy had done, that she was falling under their spell, allowing herself to be broken down and rebuilt into a sex slave zombie to be sold to the highest bidder?

She was helpless and defenseless, without power or allies. He wasn't really offering her a choice. He was inviting her to comply—or else. Was it worth another beating? Could she bear another cut of that vicious cane? If she let him have his way, as he would with or without her permission, she'd be released that much sooner, at least she hoped she would. Her hands were tingling and her back ached from maintaining this arched position. The ropes had chafed her wrists and ankles when she tried to twist away from the beating.

She closed her eyes briefly, seeing the image of Sandy as she ducked her head and smiled coquettishly for Stephen as he spewed his toxic bullshit at her. If Sandy could do it, so could Julianna. She saw the spark of fire in Sandy's eyes as they shared their secret moment when Stephen's back was turned. It wasn't buckling under or giving in, she told herself. It was surviving until she figured out a plan.

She opened her eyes and faced her tormentor. "Yes, please, sir. Let's try it again."

Anders leaned down and kissed her softly on the lips. "You please me, Julianna. I knew you were teachable. It will be a privilege to harness your passion. I almost wish *I* could—" He cut himself off and shook his head. "Never mind."

He lowered his head, taking her nipple between his lips and pulling it erect. He did the same with the other before moving down her body, licking his way toward her sex. She squirmed, very uncomfortable with the idea of such intimate contact, not that she had a choice in the matter.

When his tongue touched her pussy, she jumped slightly. He placed a hand on either thigh, holding her still as he began to lick with long, gentle strokes of his tongue. She couldn't deny that his touch soothed the sting still lingering from the cane. After a while it did more than soothe. She sighed, the pleasure rising in her loins, along with the fear that he would somehow turn this into another "teaching moment" that ended with her crying in pain.

It felt good. He pulled at her thighs, causing her labia to spread wider as he flicked at her sensitive clit with his tongue. She groaned, aware she was going to climax, frightened of what would happen next. "Please, sir," she gasped. "Can I come?"

He lifted his head long enough to say, "Not yet. Hold on for me a little longer."

Julianna squeezed her eyes shut and tried to shift beneath his touch to ease the direct attention to her throbbing clit. She thought about Stephen, letting her rage seethe and bubble. It worked. The orgasm receded like a wave ebbing from the shore.

He continued to lick and tease her, slipping two fingers into her opening. Again the orgasm mounted and again she begged, "Please sir, can I come? Please!" He didn't answer, but kept tonguing her with relentless attention, his fingers working their magic inside her.

"Please!" she cried. "I can't..." This time the orgasm rose with such strength inside her there was no way to stop it. Maybe he'd given permission and she just hadn't heard. Oh god, she couldn't help it. She was going to come. She was sweating and straining, trying to hold on, desperate for that one word that would let her give in to the onslaught.

"Please, sir..." she gasped but still there was no response.

And then she was coming, her body jerking in spasm after spasm that lifted her from the pillows. Still he didn't stop, his tongue moving rapidly as he held her fast with his strong hands. Helpless and nearly senseless, Julianna ground against Anders' tongue, all fear, all thought, obliterated in the face of the most powerful orgasm she had ever experienced in her life.

Finally he let her go. Julianna lay panting, her chest heaving, her body covered in a sheen of sweat. What was going to happen now? He had trapped her again. She had tried to obey—she had asked for permission and held off when he'd refused. He'd tricked her and now he was going to hurt her, to punish her. It was all a setup, designed so she would fail.

She felt the lift on the bed as Anders got to his feet. "You taste like honey and cinnamon," he said, as if they were lovers. He bent to release the knots at her wrists and then moved down to her ankles. When she was free of the rope, Julianna curled in on herself. She had meant to stay quiet but found herself blurting, "Please don't hurt me again. I'm sorry I came. I asked, but you didn't answer. I asked and I asked. I tried—"

"Shh." Anders sat on the bed beside Julianna and put two fingers over her lips. "It's okay. I didn't want to stop, not even long enough to say yes. You are forgiven. It wasn't your fault. I wanted to make you come. I wanted to see how far I could take you. Your passion is thrilling. You give completely of yourself, even in the most difficult of circumstances. It's almost a shame that—"

What had he been going to say? She didn't dare ask, vastly relieved he wasn't going to hit her again. She heard a beeping sound and Anders reached into his pocket and pulled out a small pager. "Seems I've lost track of time. Jay is waiting to take you for your lesson in comportment."

~*~

The day was warm and sunny, a fresh sea breeze gently moving over them. Here she was on this gorgeous tropical island for how many days, and she'd barely seen the light of day—only allowed out when being moved from one torture to the next.

Lessons in comportment didn't sound so bad, though Julianna had no real idea what this would involve. Jay led Julianna by a leash attached to her collar across the compound. At least he didn't jerk her along, but let her walk at a reasonable pace, the leash slack between them. She realized as they walked that she was no longer embarrassed about being kept naked. She didn't like it, but the constant blushes had faded. This was simply how things were.

Jay led her to a sort of open-air pavilion, a makeshift floor created with palm fronds neatly woven together beneath a large canvas tarp stretched over high poles set in a circle. There was a small raised stage on one side, with several rows of folding chairs in front of it. A woman with dark skin and hair in a white silk dress awaited them, and when they were close enough, Julianna saw that it was Alma.

Her face lit up upon seeing them, which confused Julianna until she realized Alma had eyes only for Jay. Their exchanged look was a kind of embrace, though no words passed between them.

Jay unclipped the leash and stepped back. He turned one of the chairs to face the women and sat down, stretching out his legs and putting his hands behind his head. Alma turned her attention to Julianna. "You are okay?" she asked, touching Julianna's shoulder.

Julianna glanced to Jay and back to Alma, not sure what new trap this was. "Oh," Alma said. "No cameras out here. It's safe to talk."

"But..." Julianna's glance darted again toward Jay, who had leaned his head back and closed his eyes. She hoped he stayed that way, not eager to have him watch whatever these comportment lessons turned out to be.

"It's okay. Jay is a good man. He won't say anything. We—we have an understanding."

Julianna didn't know what to say to this. She recalled now that brief but bright smile the two had exchanged at her bungalow, the only real smiles she'd seen on this godforsaken island, and now their shared look of love. Yes, it was the look of lovers. But that made no sense. How could Alma, clearly kept on the island against her will, have fallen in love with one of her captors?

Alma again touched Julianna's shoulder. "I know your number, but I don't know your name." She said it almost shyly, and smiled.

Julianna felt a small, fierce rush of gratitude at the question. "Julianna," she said, savoring the syllables. She was not a number. She was Julianna Beckett.

Alma nodded, repeating the name in her lilting accent. "You look well. They are feeding you? You are adapting?"

A small hysterical laugh welled up in Julianna's throat. "I look *well*?" Julianna tugged at the thick leather collar around her neck and then wrapped her arms around her naked body. "I guess, for being half-starved and kept prisoner and tortured every waking moment, I'm just fine and dandy." She heard the bitterness in her own voice. She put a hand over her mouth, hardly able to believe she'd just said that out loud with Jay only a few feet away, but Alma only smiled sadly and nodded.

"I am sorry. You are right. I forget sometimes there is a world beyond this place. It almost has come to seem normal now, the only life I know. Until Jay came—" She glanced at the man, not finishing her sentence.

Julianna's curiosity was piqued. "Until Jay came…" she prompted. When Alma didn't answer, she ventured, "You aren't, uh, for sale? I mean, not like the other women here. Like me." *Like me. For sale.* I'm *for sale. How fucking bizarre is that?*

Alma shook her head. "No. I used to belong to Jason. But he," she lowered her head, sadness moving over her face, "grew tired of me. Now I serve all the men on the island, and help with some of the training of the new girls."

I used to belong to Jason. Before Julianna could probe further, she heard someone approaching from behind them and whirled to see Anders, broad shouldered and smiling, his golden hair glinting in the sun. Jay sat up abruptly in his chair at Anders' approach and leaned forward, his hands now resting on his knees, his expression alert.

The lines of Alma's face fell into a bland sort of calm. She dipped her head gracefully toward Anders. "Good afternoon, sir."

"Hello, Alma." He moved toward Jay and, grabbing one of the chairs, pulled it alongside the other man and sat. "I found myself with a little free time and thought I'd watch the lesson."

"We were just getting started," Alma said. She turned to Julianna. "Today we will focus on walking and kneeling. If we have time, we'll cover a few of the basic positions as well."

"Come over here," Anders called. "Have her do it in front of us to keep her properly motivated."

Julianna saw the briefest flash of irritation move over Alma's face, a tiny ripple in the calm, but when she turned toward him she was smiling and again dipped her head submissively. "Yes, sir, as you wish."

Taking Julianna gently by the arm, she led her to stand in front of the men. Jay's eyes were on Alma, which suited Julianna just fine, but Anders was gazing at her, his eyes moving over her body like a caress. She felt herself flushing and looked down.

There was a shoebox on the ground nearby. Alma took out a pair of very high heels, which Julianna regarded with dismay. She took Julianna's hands to support her as she reluctantly stepped into them. "The key here," Alma began, "is to get used to the new positioning of your weight in the shoes. Stand still for a while and then turn slightly to each side."

Julianna tried to obey, feeling ridiculous in front of the men, naked save for the high heels. Alma put a hand on Julianna's lower back. "Posture is crucial. Stand straight and proud. Good. Now you will take a few steps. Keep your legs as straight as possible and close together. Start off with slow, short steps, placing your heel down first and then rolling onto the flat of your foot, the ball and then your toes."

Julianna tried to follow the complicated instructions, wobbling forward. "Not too bad," Alma said.

"Remember to swing your arms as you walk. This will help you to keep your balance. With each step, point your feet as straight in front of you as you can."

She took one of Julianna's hands and began to lead her back and forth in front of the men, keeping up a running commentary as she went. Julianna had no idea there was so much involved in just walking in a pair of fucking shoes. "Remember, the more relaxed you are, the easier it will be to keep your balance. Back straight, head up, and round out those shoulders. That's it. Good. Very good."

Finally Alma let her take off the shoes, which had pinched her toes into an uncomfortable V. "Next, we'll work on kneeling," Alma said.

"Take off your dress so she can see the positions better," Anders interjected. Julianna thought she detected a faint flush move over Alma's tan skin, but she didn't hesitate as she lifted the white dress over her head, revealing her naked body.

She had heavy breasts, the nipples large and brown above a short but slender waist that flared into generous hips. She, like all the women on the island, was shaven smooth. She seemed to take no notice at all of the men staring at them, completely focused on Julianna and their task. Julianna tried to imitate this behavior, but her eyes kept flitting toward the men, who watched them, Julianna thought, like slavering dogs waiting for their bones.

Julianna tried to copy Alma's positions as she demonstrated various ways to kneel. Alma was so elegant and graceful, as fluid as a swan gliding on a lake, while Julianna felt awkward and clumsy beside her. The whole thing was made much worse by Anders' presence. He was watching her so intently. She wondered worriedly if he was keeping some kind of score for which she would be punished later. It was hard to concentrate. She was hot and thirsty. Her muscles were growing tired and her temper growing short.

Suddenly they heard men shouting nearby and all four of them turned to see what the commotion was. "She stabbed me! That fucking cunt stabbed me! With my own goddamn pen, she stabbed me!" Vince lurched into view, his hand clutched over his left thigh, blood spurting between his fingers. Anders and Jay leaped up. "Number fucking thirty-one, that little bitch," Vince whined. "She took off into the ocean! Get her!"

Anders nodded toward Jay, his voice tense. "Send out an all-alert bulletin on your walkie-talkie and get the boat. Make sure Jason knows. I'll stay with the girls." Jay looked at Alma, who gave the tiniest of nods. Her eyes were wide with fear.

Number thirty-one. Sandy!

Vince collapsed onto one of the chairs and Anders crouched beside him, examining the gash on his thigh. Julianna stared at them, thinking of the petite waif of a girl, wondering how she had managed to get the pen from Vince's hand, thinking how hard she had to ram it into his leg to create that wound. Before this, back in that other life when she'd taken the occasional self-defense course, they'd always said the best thing was to get away. Run! She'd liked this approach, squeamish at the thought of actually hurting someone else. But that was before she'd truly learned what rage felt like. She knew now, if she'd been the one with the pen and the chance, she wouldn't have gone for Vince's leg. She would have plunged that pen right into his eye, gouging it out without the slightest hesitation.

She stared at the big, stupid oaf of a man, who was still cursing and whining. "Stupid, fucking cunt," she heard him mutter. "When I get my hands on her..."

Silently Alma touched Julianna's arm and using her body as a shield from the men, pointed between the palms toward the shore and the ocean beyond. Julianna peered out, her heart giving a wild jolt at the sight of a small blond head bobbing in the current. Sandy was swimming out to sea!

In the distance, Julianna could hear the sound of the boat's engine.

"She won't make it," Alma whispered, her eyes filling with tears.

Never give up.

Go, Sandy, go! Never give up! The words rose like a cheer in Julianna's throat and she had to bite down on her lip to keep from shouting them aloud. *Fuck you, Stephen! Fuck you, Jason! Fuck you all!* Julianna had no idea how far other land might be, or if there was any way in hell Sandy would make it alive. Maybe a boat or ship would spot her and pull her to safety before these monster set out to track her down. *Go, Sandy. Swim hard. You can do it Never give up!*

Whatever happened, for this moment in time, one of them had beaten the system—she'd beaten them all. The tiny shoot of hope that had burrowed its way through Julianna's fears flowered at that moment, all of that hope focused on the brave young woman swimming away from this wretched place, against all odds.

Julianna took Alma's hand as they watched Sandy disappear from view.

Chapter 9

Anders used his walkie-talkie and a minute later Jorge and Pete appeared. They took Julianna back to the slave quarters, hustling her quickly along. As they went, Julianna could see Jason and Stephen standing on the shore, their hands raised to shield their eyes as they scanned the ocean for the missing girl. Jay's boat was moving in a wide circle over the water.

As the men led her along the corridor of the slave quarters, Julianna decided to take a chance. She didn't know if the guards knew what was going on or not. Somehow she suspected these two hadn't been clued in. She whispered, "It's Sandy. Uh, number thirty-one. She got away!"

She watched as the two usually implacable faces suddenly showed a spark of real interest. They looked at each other and then at her and she was pretty sure they hadn't known until that moment. Her growing feeling that these two men were also slaves of some kind on the island strengthened. She waited, hoping they would say something, offer a bit of information, show that they cared or even that they didn't. Something. But that spark passing between them was all she got before the masks were lowered again.

These were big, strong men! Why did they allow themselves to be used and controlled? What hold did

Jason have over them? They seemed to come and go freely on the island. Was her gut wrong? Were they there of their own free will? Did they enjoy what they did? Did they get paid well to do it?

Without a word, they led Julianna to the closest empty cell. As Jorge opened the barred door, she tried again. "Do you think she'll make it? She looked pretty far away when I saw her. Does she have a chance?"

"You talk too much," Jorge said. "Silence is better." The door shut with a clang and the scraping of the lock, and then they hurried off. She realized with a small shock that they hadn't even taken the time to chain her to the bed. They must have been more affected by the news of Sandy's escape than they let on.

She moved toward the door, gripping the bars and trying to see down the hall, but there was nothing to see. She could hear a woman nearby crying softly. *How many of us are there here,* she wondered. There were eight cells in total, but she had only seen two or three occupied at any given time. How many men were on the island? Anders, Stephen, Jason, Vince, Jay and the two guards. How quickly did they move the women in and out? She was number thirty-eight, and Sandy, thirty-one, had still been on the island, meaning there could be as many as eight women there, though some might have been sold in the interim.

Sold…or worse. Maybe Sandy wasn't the first to escape. Or the first to die trying. What would happen to her if they caught her?

With a deep shudder, Julianna sat on her bed. She was hungry and thirsty, but she had grown used to that. She lay down and stared at the ceiling, mentally going over the setup of Stephen's torture chamber and Ander's training room. What was in there that she could get hold of? She knew she wouldn't hesitate to attack Stephen, but what about Anders?

There was the sound of footsteps and masculine voices. The cell beside hers clanged open. "Let's go," she heard Jorge say. After a few moments, he moved to Julianna's cell, unlocking the door and pulling it open.

"Let's go," Jorge said again, and Julianna stepped out, knowing she had no choice. Jorge and Pete had with them a naked woman in her early twenties. She had honey blond, curly hair and large, round breasts over a long, slender body. Her face would have been beautiful, but it was twisted and drawn by fear. Her hands were cuffed on either side of her collar and her ankles were hobbled with cuffs, a short length of chain between them. Just as Julianna had assigned the name Sandy to number thirty-one, she decided to call this girl Ashley. They would never be numbers, not to her.

The men cuffed Julianna's wrists to her collar and hobbled her ankles as they'd done with Ashley. They attached a chain between the two girls, tethering them together by the O-rings on their collars, Julianna standing behind Ashley. They led them down to the next occupied cell, where a petite girl with short dark hair sat huddled on her cot.

She, like Sandy, looked barely out of her teens. She had a woman's body, but her cheeks still carried a hint of childhood roundness. Her eyes were puffy and red, tears staining her face. She must have been the one Julianna heard crying. *Rachel,* Julianna decided. She wanted to take the poor girl in her arms and tell her everything would be okay, but of course, things weren't okay, and might never be again.

Rachel was cuffed and hobbled in similar fashion and then attached behind Julianna. A fourth girl was added, tall and statuesque, with dark eyes and raven black hair that fell in a shiny curtain down her back. *Veronica.*

With Jorge at the head and Pete at the rear, the four women were led out of the quarters and into the bright sunlight. Rachel was still sniffling. As the men led them outside, Julianna realized she was clenching her jaw so tight that it ached. They were brought to the pavilion where Alma had given her the lessons. Alma was gone, as was Vince, but Stephen and Jason were there, both of them with tight, angry expressions. Jason was holding a long, thin cane in his hands.

Stephen directed the guards to unclip the girls from each other. They were kept hobbled, their arms chained to their collars. "Kneel up." He pointed to the ground and all four girls lowered themselves, facing him in a line. He looked slowly from one to the next, his eyes blazing with barely concealed rage. Julianna stole a glance at Jason, who looked just as furious.

She must have got away, Julianna thought, suddenly exultant. *That's why they're so pissed.*

"Stop sniveling, thirty-six!" With a sudden, sharp movement, Stephen reached down and slapped Rachel hard across the face. The girl gasped, then hiccupped, tears still rolling down her cheeks.

Fucking bastard, Julianna thought furiously. She stared at the ground, trying to get her own expression under control so it wouldn't betray her rage. She realized the other girls probably had no clue that one of them had managed to escape.

Stephen stood back, crossing his arms over his chest. "We have brought you out here to conduct a little experiment. You are each at different stages in your training, but I'm going to give you a chance to prove your submission and obedience. It's one thing to passively submit to what's done to you. It's possible to pretend with the body when the heart is not engaged. It's possible to fool even the most discerning Master."

A spasm of pain moved over Stephen's face as he said this. Julianna flashed back to the almost fond way he had looked at Sandy when he talked to her, the tender way he had stroked her head, and his proud declaration that she had not only accepted but embraced her "fate". Clearly he must be referring now to Sandy, to her pretending to submit when her "heart wasn't engaged".

Was the man really that fucking deluded? Did he actually think he could torture and brainwash human beings into not only submitting to his sadistic will, but to loving him for it? Whatever his twisted thinking, it was clear Stephen had, in his own mind at least, been burned. *Fuck you, Stephen,* she thought for the thousandth time.

"Today I'm going to give each of you the opportunity to *actively* prove your submission and devotion to me, your trainer. If you please me, you will be rewarded. If you fail, you will suffer the consequences." He turned to Jason. "The cane, please."

Jason handed him the cane. Stephen tapped the blonde's shoulder with the tip of it. "Stand up, thirty-four." She obeyed, her large blue eyes wide with fear. He released her wrists from her collar. "We'll start with you. I want you to beat number thirty-three. Leave marks. Prove your submission."

He held the cane out to her and Ashley took it hesitantly. Stephen grabbed Veronica by her elbows and pulled her to her feet. "You will show your submission by accepting the caning with grace, and thanking number thirty-four afterwards."

"Yes, sir," the girl said in a meek voice.

He positioned Ashley beside Veronica. "Ten strokes. Hard. I want to see welts."

Ashley looked helplessly at him and then at the cane in her hands. "Please, sir, I don't—"

"Silence! I didn't ask you to speak. Do as you're told. *Now.*"

Her hand trembling, Ashley lifted the cane and batted rather ineffectually at Veronica's voluptuous ass.

Julianna saw it was already marked with fading lines of purple and black.

"You can do better than that, thirty-four." Stephen voice was soft, but menacing. Ashley hit the girl harder, a long, red line appearing over both cheeks. Stephen had Veronica count as each stroke marked her flesh. Ashley seemed to grow in confidence as she struck the other woman, each time a little harder than the last.

When she was done, Veronica, who had barely whimpered, turned and knelt, lowering herself gracefully to kiss the top of Ashley's bare foot. "Thank you, ma'am, for using this worthless slave."

Stephen actually applauded, while Jason laughed. The two guards stood stony-faced as usual. "Excellent." Stephen moved toward them, taking the cane from Ashley. He re-cuffed her wrists at her collar while Jason released Veronica's cuffs.

"Now, thirty-three. Return the favor. Show thirty-four how it's done. Don't hold back." He handed the cane to Veronica. Julianna saw a cruel gleam in the girl's eye. Ashley, whose entire body had started to tremble, was directed to turn around and stay still.

"Don't forget to count," Stephen admonished.

The first blow landed hard, the loud thwack of the cane against flesh making both Rachel and Julianna jump. Ashley cried out and then gasped, "One!" Veronica hit her with hard, methodical strokes. On the fifth stroke, she hit her thighs, raising a long, ugly welt horizontally across both legs. Ashley screamed in pain and stumbled forward in her chains.

Veronica continued to whip her, the last blow landing with a vicious cut across Ashley's shoulders. Ashley collapsed to the ground. Julianna could barely believe what she was witnessing. Veronica's expression was one of triumph. She tossed her hair and simpered at Stephen. Stephen moved close, stroking her cheek. Julianna saw the erection bulging in his pants and looked away with disgust and fury.

Jason, meanwhile, prodded the crying girl with the toe of his shoe. "Thank her." Ashley turned, still on her knees, and lowered her face to Veronica's foot. She kissed it, mumbling the words she was forced to say. Julianna's heart ached for the girl. Veronica had given her a vicious beating, much harder than the one she'd received.

Once they'd forced the two girls back into the line, Julianna gulped as Stephen moved toward her and Rachel. He pulled Rachel to her feet and unclipped her cuffs. Handing her the cane, he said, "Show your worth."

He pulled Julianna up and positioned her so her back was toward little Rachel. The first blow wasn't very hard. "One!" Julianna shouted.

"Harder!" Stephen commanded. The second stroke was harder. It hurt, but it wasn't unbearable. She counted as each stinging stroke cut across her skin. "Harder. Show me your devotion." Julianna was caught unprepared for the slice of the cane as it struck her lower back, searing her like a brand.

"Oh god! I'm sorry! I missed," Rachel cried.

"Stupid girl!" Stephen grabbed the cane from Rachel and pushed her to the ground. "I'll finish this. You're useless." He hit Julianna four more times, each harder than the last, cutting across her ass, thighs and back. He pressed her shoulder. It didn't take much for her to sink to her knees.

"Thank me properly."

Julianna managed to kneel down and touch her lips to Stephen's sandal. "Thank-you-sir-for-using-this-worthless-slave." She said it in a rapid monotone, the words strung together as if they were little more than nonsense syllables.

Stephen jerked her arm, pulling her to her feet. He spun her around, releasing the clips on her cuffs and thrusting the cane into her hands. Julianna, her back and ass stinging, looked down at Rachel, who was curled into a ball on the ground, sobbing.

How could she hit this girl, this child? She glanced at Veronica and Ashley, both of whom were looking at the ground, no doubt relieved they were no longer in the spotlight. She looked at Jorge and Pete and saw they were looking at each other, as if blocking out what was going on before them. Stealing a glance at Jason, she saw he was stroking his crotch, a small, mean smile on his face.

Stephen hauled Rachel to her feet and positioned her away from Julianna. "Beat this useless slave," he ordered Julianna. "Show her no mercy. Give her ten good ones. I want to see blood."

Jesus. *Blood!* She had no idea how to handle a cane, but couldn't imagine hitting someone hard enough to draw blood. Just the thought of it made her feel sick. There was no way Julianna could do this. Yet she knew if she didn't, Stephen would take over and do it for her.

Taking a deep breath, she let the cane fall against Rachel's small ass. The girl whimpered and said, "One."

"Harder," Stephen said.

With a silent apology, Julianna struck the girl again, a little harder. "Two!"

"Harder!" Stephen barked.

Julianna obeyed, her heart wrenching when the girl gasped and yelped. The third line rose dark and angry just below the first two. Julianna felt faint, her ears ringing. "Go on," Stephen commanded. "Another. Mark her thighs. Strike her back. Make her suffer. Make her bleed. Do it, number thirty-eight, or pay the price."

A small, dark voice whispered in her head. *Do it. Just do it. Save yourself. You have no choice. It's you or her.* It wasn't her doing it—it was Stephen. He was forcing her to, with his henchmen and bullies around him. If she didn't comply, he'd probably hurt Rachel even more, and then turn his vicious wrath on her. She had no choice. She had to do this.

I'm so sorry, Rachel, she whispered in her head. Julianna pulled back her arm and flicked her wrist, the cane whooshing through the air. At the moment of impact, Rachel screamed and jerked sideways, causing the cane to wrap around her torso, leaving a long, ugly welt in its wake. Droplets of blood appeared along the welted line on Rachel's thin body. Julianna stared, horrified at what she had done.

Rachel collapsed to the ground, curling up like a terrified animal. Julianna couldn't remember ever feeling more wretched in her life. A slow, cold fury rose in her gut, along with the nausea.

"Go on. You're not done." Stephen's words cut like a razorblade.

Jason forced Rachel again to her feet. Julianna's heart was beating too hard, too fast. She felt like she was going to pass out. Nothing she'd suffered so far on this wretched island had been as bad as this. It was one thing to suffer, quite another to be the direct cause of someone else's agony. She couldn't strike the poor girl again.

Julianna clenched the handle of the cane. Her hands were slick with sweat. She knew she had no choice. Her body felt sluggish. She couldn't seem to control her movements. It was a like a bad dream where you try to run, but find your legs are stuck in place.

She could feel Stephen's will, like a magnetic current moving over her, forcing her to do what he wanted. She lifted the cane, but again she hesitated. She couldn't beat this young girl, not again. Not even if it meant terrible punishment.

They could control her body—they could starve her, beat her, even kill her. But by forcing her into the role of aggressor, by making her complicit in their cowardly, cruel games, they had tried to steal and desecrate that part of her that kept her human. They would not, they could not, have her soul.

The cane clattered from her fingers to the ground.

"Pick. It. Up."

She let her hand fall to her side and straightened up. Though she was shaking with fear, she looked directly into Stephen's cold gray eyes, thrusting out her chin in defiance.

"No."

Chapter 10

At a look from Stephen, the guards dragged Rachel back into the line of kneeling girls. Stephen turned his cold, hard gaze on Julianna. Barely contained fury sparked behind them. What had she done? What would he do to her? Would the other men just stand by and let him kill her?

Stephen turned from her, speaking now to the line of girls kneeling in a row. "It is quite clear," he said, his voice dripping venom, "that this worthless slave needs to be taught a lesson. A very firm lesson. I trust the rest of you will learn by her example, what happens to girls who say no."

His head swiveled toward the guards. "Hold her in position, arms fully extended." Jorge and Pete moved to stand in front of Julianna. Each took hold of a wrist, pulling Julianna's arms until they were stretched out on either side of her. Stephen stood behind her, the cane in his hand.

Terror broke over Julianna like a cold sweat. If the guards hadn't been holding her upright, she would have fallen. Stephen leaned close, his hot breath on her neck. "I never met a girl yet who I couldn't break." He stepped back.

The first blow struck hard across her ass. Julianna yelped and jerked but the men held her in place.

Stephen chose a spot on one cheek, striking it over and over until Julianna thought it must literally be on fire. She was screaming, struggling hard against the strong hands that held her in place as she tried in vain to avoid the relentless cut of the cane.

Her mind began to fog with pain. She felt the warm trickle of something down her leg and realized it must be blood. Her head fell forward, her legs giving out.

"Hold her up," Stephen snapped.

The men each took hold of one of her upper arms, pulling her upright and supporting her weight. Mercifully the cane shifted at last, now, now painting lines of stinging fire over her back, ass and thighs. Each time she swore she couldn't take another stroke, another landed, and then another. The air was filled with a high-pitched, keening cry. She was dimly aware it was her own voice though the sound seemed disembodied, floating somewhere over her head.

Strong fingers gripped her arms as she sagged. Pain washed through her—long, searing stripes of white hot pain. *I can't do this. I can't take this.* And yet she did. On and on it went, until her nerve endings, mercifully, began to numb.

She could still hear the sound of the cane cutting through the air and landing across her skin but she couldn't feel it any longer. Her body was icy, as if her very blood had frozen in its veins. Her lungs felt like balloons that had lost all their air. She was breathing fast and hard, but no oxygen seemed to be reaching her. A rushing sound thundered through her ears, blotting out all other sound, as a gray, cold mist moved over her eyes, blinding her.

"Thank god," she whispered, letting the darkness take her.

~*~

Julianna opened her eyes. It was dark and she had no idea where she was. She tried to move, but realized she was immobilized, her wrists pulled over her head and chained to the wall. She was standing upright, held in place by manacles at her wrists and ankles, as well as a thick band of leather secured around her waist.

The air was warm and close, and she recognized the fetid stench of the solitary confinement hut. Her back was against the wall, her skin still tender and stinging. She jerked forward, trying to wrench herself free, but only succeeded in nearly choking herself on her collar. She let her head fall back, too exhausted and defeated even to cry.

~*~

When next Julianna opened her eyes, the hut was suffused with the pale gray light of dawn. It felt like there was sand in her eyes but she could do nothing but blink. Her whole body felt gritty with the stuff and she longed for a shower. Her arms were numb. She tried to move her fingers but had no idea if she was succeeding. She needed to pee. She desperately wanted to close her legs to alleviate some of the pressure in her bladder, but chained as she was, she could not. She listened hard for a while, trying to tell if anyone was out there, if anyone was coming for her.

She squirmed and felt a few drops of urine escape. She knew she was seconds away from losing control. "Oh, shit," she cursed, as all at once the floodgates opened. She couldn't deny the physical relief she felt as the hot stream splashed between her legs, puddling on the floor at her feet.

To think she'd been reduced to this—naked and filthy, forced to stand in a puddle of her own urine, chained to the wall like a character in some medieval nightmare. Humiliation fought with anger at the thought of the men walking in and seeing her like this.

Anger won.

I never met a girl yet who I couldn't break.

Julianna stoked her anger on those words. "Fuck you, Stephen," she muttered, letting the rage move through her like an ocean wave. "You didn't break Sandy. You won't break me." Closing her eyes, she fell again into a fitful doze, dreaming of the vast ocean meeting the endless sky, a tiny blond head bobbing in the distance.

When next she awoke, it was from the heat. She could feel the sweat rolling down her sides and between her breasts. The collar around her neck chafed at her damp, itchy skin. Her hair was matted and tangled, and an annoying strand kept falling into her face. A bead of sweat slipped into her eyes, stinging like mad.

Her heart began to thump at the sound of the ATV approaching. The door swung outward and Jorge came in. Pete entered just behind him, a tall, thin silhouette against a blinding rectangle of sunlight.

When Julianna's eyes adjusted to the brightness, she saw the canteen in Jorge's hand. "Water," she croaked. She licked her cracked, chapped lips, her eyes glued to the canteen, her heart leaping with anticipation.

Unscrewing the cap, he held the canteen to her mouth and tipped it. Julianna drank, deeply grateful for the cool water. She felt like a shriveled, drooping plant being restored as the water coursed down her throat. He let her drink her fill. Nothing had ever tasted as fresh or pure. While she drank, he watched her with those dark, somber eyes.

Pete came up alongside Jorge. Together they released her limbs from the manacles. If they noticed the puddle of pee that had seeped into the floorboards, they made no mention of it, for which Julianna was grateful. Jorge lifted Julianna into his arms as she flopped forward against him.

He laid her on the cot and sat beside her, rubbing at her arms with both hands. They began to tingle painfully back to life, moving from cold to hot as the blood rushed in. Her back muscles spasmed and she gasped from the pain.

"You'll be okay," Jorge offered, which coming from him was effusive concern. "Move your fingers."

Julianna complied, and was relieved to see they seemed to be working fine. Carefully he rolled her over, running a rough finger over the welts. "Pete, bring the water bucket."

When Pete had complied, Jorge pulled a bandana from his back pocket and dunked it into the water. "It's not too bad," he said, as he ran the damp cloth over her skin. "The only real wound is here." He touched her left cheek where Stephen had struck over and over on a single spot. Julianna jumped with pain as he washed the area, flinching and squeezing her eyes shut.

He dunked the rag again, focusing on the rest of her body. "The skin's not cut on your back and thighs—the welts are already fading. You might end up with a scar on your ass, though."

Julianna didn't want think about this. Instead she asked, "What about Rach—er, the dark-haired girl? Did Stephen hurt her?"

Jorge frowned. "She's okay." Julianna waited for him to continue, but he said nothing more.

When he was done washing her off, he dropped the bandana into the bucket and stood. "Jason wants you." Julianna's gut clenched at this declaration. Jason wanted her. She didn't even want to think for what.

The men helped her to sit up and then stand. She was at once assailed with dizziness and sat back heavily on the cot, sucking in her breath sharply as the cut skin on her ass made contact with the rough canvas. Pete reached into his pocket and pulled out a rather bruised banana. He looked at Jorge with a question in his eyes. Jorge shrugged and nodded.

Pete peeled the banana and handed the yellow fruit to Julianna. She took it, half afraid it was some kind of trick, but he just stood impassively as usual, his hands in his pockets as he watched her. Before he could change his mind, Julianna began to gobble the overripe banana, chewing and swallowing as fast as she could. Jorge handed her the canteen, allowing her to drink from it herself.

Julianna had a sudden, horrible premonition this was her "last supper". Why else were they being so kind to her? She was to be taken to Jason. Jason wasn't a trainer. He was the owner of the island—the man who ultimately called the shots. Was she going to be sold? After her refusal to beat Rachel, had Stephen decided she was of no use to them any longer? Was she going to be handed off to pimps, whored out on the streets of some third world country? Terror gripped her innards and the banana lay like a heavy lump in her stomach.

I have to get out before that happens. I have *to get away.*

Jorge took the canteen from her and attached it to his belt. "We're taking you first to Alma's. She'll get you cleaned up." *Alma!* Julianna felt a surge of hope. Alma would know what was going on, maybe even help her.

Julianna stood on her own, feeling weak but otherwise fine, save for the throbbing spot on her bottom where that bastard had cut the skin. She touched the area and felt the fragile scabbing. Hatred moved through her like corroding acid as she unwillingly relived the scene, recalling her own terror, and that of poor Rachel, huddled and crying on the ground.

The men drove her to Alma's bungalow, sandwiched between them on the ATV. She held herself gingerly on the seat, angled so the wound didn't touch the leather. Alma opened her door as they were pulling up, apparently expecting her. Julianna was relieved when the men didn't enter the bungalow as Alma led her inside. "Thirty minutes," Jorge said, and Alma nodded and shut the door.

After the dark squalor of the hut, the room seemed so fresh and clean, with its white walls, and a large fan oscillating in the corner. The little bed was made, the edge of fresh white sheets folded neatly over a thin blue coverlet. Julianna longed to sink down onto it and sleep for a hundred years. When she awoke, every man on this island would be long dead. If this were a fairytale, that is. She sighed.

Alma, who every other time she'd seen her had always seemed so placid, even serene, now looked deeply troubled. Julianna's sense of foreboding increased tenfold. "What's going to happen to me?" she whispered urgently. Alma shook her head, pressing her lips together. Julianna felt panic rising like a tide. She took a deep breath, trying to keep herself together.

Alma led her to the shower and turned it on, gesturing for Julianna to enter. She stood gratefully beneath the water, just letting it splash over her as she took long, deep breaths, willing herself to calm down. At least, she told herself, it wasn't Stephen who had sent for her. It was Jason. Again her mind landed on and then veered away from what he might want with her.

She reached for the shampoo, washing her hair and rinsing it, and then washing it again. She squirted a large dollop of conditioner on her palm and ran it through the tangles, her fingers recalling the many heads of the ladies she washed back at Sophie's Salon.

That world no longer seemed real. It was a dream—a longed for fantasy that might never come true again, at least not for her.

She shook her head, telling herself this kind of thinking had no place in her mind or heart. New York was real. The life she had left behind was real. She was real—a real person with dreams, hopes and the right to live freely. She wasn't a number, she wasn't a slave and she wasn't done fighting.

She reached for the soap, which stung her welted skin, but it felt so good to clean the sweat, grime and filth from her body. She lingered as long as she dared. Pulling back the curtain, Julianna grabbed the towel Alma had left for her and looked around the bungalow.

She didn't see Alma at first. "Alma?" she called softly, confused and frightened to find herself alone. She scanned the room and saw a shadow behind the rice-paper screen in the corner of the bungalow. She hurried toward it, peering around the edge. The space was set up as a small kitchen. Alma stood there, her face in her hands, her shoulders shaking.

Shocked, Julianna moved quickly to her. "Alma, what is it?"

Alma looked up, wiping her eyes and sniffing. "I'm sorry," she whispered. "I can't help it. I only just got the horrible news."

Julianna clenched her hands into fists, nearly faint with fear, certain now she was going to be sold to pimps. Alma began to cry again and whispered in a choked voice, "Jason sold me. I'm to leave the island in two weeks."

Julianna stared. She'd been so absorbed and focused on herself, it hadn't occurred to her Alma might have problems as bad as her own. "What? Sold *you*?" Julianna blurted.

Alma put her finger to her lips. "Shh, they'll hear you," she whispered. "The camera can't see past the screen but the microphone is sensitive. If we whisper very softly from here, they have a hard time hearing. Especially with the fan on."

Julianna nodded. There was a tiny table with a chair on either side. Alma sat and gestured for Julianna to do the same. It felt at once strange and exhilarating to be invited to sit down at a table, as if she were a regular person. She wrapped her bath towel tighter, thrilled not to be naked, though she knew it wouldn't last.

She thought about Alma and "the understanding" she'd said she and Jay shared. "Does Jay know?" she whispered.

Alma began to cry again. She shook her head. "I haven't seen him yet to tell him. It could be I won't be allowed to see him alone again, now that the decision has been made. He and Vince are just hired hands. They don't live on the island like the others."

Julianna nodded. Whatever understanding Jay and Alma might have, how far could it go anyway? Alma was an island slave, used by all the men, as much a prisoner as Julianna herself, even if she was allowed certain superficial freedoms. Why would Jay bother to risk his job or maybe even his life to help her?

Then she remembered the smile they'd shared, and the way their faces lit up when they saw each other. Could love exist, even in this dark and terrifying place?

"Have you—have you met the man who's..." She couldn't even say the words. The concept of one person buying another seemed so alien, though she knew it happened all the time, in every country in the world.

Alma didn't need to hear the words. She nodded, tears again spilling. "A wealthy Colombian businessman. He already owns three girls, apparently, and wants another. *Ai, Dios mio,* I don't want to go. At least here I have some degree of freedom. I have my own place." She held her arms out. "I have...or I had... Jay."

There was a knock at the door and Alma startled, putting her hand to her mouth.

"Fifteen minutes," Jorge called, and then shut the door.

"We must hurry!" Alma jumped up, dragging Julianna into the main room. As they stood before the mirror, Alma took the towel from Julianna and examined the welts left from the caning, her fingers moving lightly over Julianna's back. "These should be gone in a day or two." Then she gasped quietly, touching Julianna's hip just above where he'd struck her repeatedly. "Ah, but this, this might scar. What was he thinking?"

Julianna twisted to look at herself. On her left cheek there was a dark purple welt, really several welts, one just above the other. The skin was split and flayed, though at least it was no longer bleeding. Feeling sick, Julianna turned back around, leaning forward and pressing her hands flat against the vanity's surface.

Alma reached into a drawer and pulled out a tube of triple antibiotic cream. "This will help." She smeared a generous amount over the welted skin, her fingers gentle. Folding the bath towel, she put it on the small stool and gestured for Julianna to sit.

Working quickly, she did Julianna's hair and makeup. She chose another of the silky white dresses for Julianna to wear, along with a dreaded pair of black high heels. She handed Julianna a skimpy pair of white lace panties.

Julianna looked at them doubtfully. "Go on, put them on," Alma said, turning away. "Jason likes to..." she trailed away. "Just put them on."

Julianna obeyed, her hands trembling as she pulled on the flimsy panties. Focusing on Alma's problems for those few minutes had given her a moment's respite from her own constant, gnawing fear, but now it had returned with a vengeance.

The door opened again, and both Jorge and Pete stepped inside. "Time to go."

Realizing this might well be the last time she ever saw Alma again, Julianna whispered quickly, "Courage," as Alma had to her that first terrifying day.

She grabbed Alma's hand and squeezed it for a moment. Alma squeezed back and then looked away.

Chapter 11

Julianna was taken to a part of the island she hadn't seen before. Two small houses stood side-by-side, built of white stucco with red clay tiled roofs. The ATV stopped in front of the one on the left. The guards had cuffed her wrists again behind her back. They led her through soft grass to the back, which faced the ocean. Julianna stumbled a little in the high heels, but the men kept steadying hands on either side of her.

Ever since the beating, Jorge and Pete had treated her differently—almost kindly. What had changed? Was it because she'd dared to say no to Stephen? Had either of them ever dared to say no?

Jason was sitting at a table beneath a large yellow umbrella, a drink in his hand, a lit cigar between his teeth. He was staring out at the sea, frowning. He looked toward them as they approached, his expression easing.

"Ah, there she is. Bring her here." The guards brought Julianna to stand in front of Jason. "Turn her around and lift her dress. I want to see what he did."

Jorge pulled on Julianna's arm and she turned. Pete lifted the hem of her dress, tucking it over her cuffed wrists. She felt the tug of the panties as they were dragged down to her thighs. As absurd as it was given all she'd been through, she felt herself blushing, feeling somehow more exposed because of the clothing than if she'd been naked.

Jason emitted a low growl as blunt fingers probed the welts. "Stupid man. What was he thinking?" he muttered to himself. He echoed Alma's words, but while Julianna believed Alma had been shocked at the brutality, she had the distinct feeling that Jason cared only about his "property" being potentially damaged.

Her panties were pulled back up and the dress dropped. "You can go, boys," Jason said. "I won't require your services tonight." Julianna saw the two men exchange a quick look before their faces smoothed into the usual stone.

As they walked away, Jason stroked the back of Julianna's leg. "Turn around. Let me see you." Julianna obeyed, the heat still in her face. Setting down his cigar, he looked her slowly over from head to toe, the tip of his tongue appearing between his lips. He brought his hands together and rubbed them. "You'll do very nicely," he said, and she couldn't stop the shudder of fear and loathing that shook her frame.

He didn't notice, or didn't care. Taking a towel from the back of his chair, he folded it in a thick square and placed it on the seat of the chair beside his. Patting it, he said, "Sit on that. I don't want those welts to bleed." He shook his head, again muttering in a voice barely audible, "Stupid man."

Julianna perched on the chair as best she could with her hands behind her back. The towel felt so soft beneath her. While she understood he wasn't doing this to be kind, but rather to protect his investment, she appreciated it nonetheless.

Her eyes were drawn to the feast spread out on the table and her mouth began to water, Pete's banana only a memory. There were plates of cut fruit and cheese, slices of bread and a mound of curled pink and white shrimp heaped in a bowl of crushed ice. There was a blue glass pitcher with sliced oranges and lemons rimming the edge, and two glasses filled with ice.

He reached for the pitcher and filled a glass. Lifting it, he asked, "Thirsty?"

"Yes, sir."

He held the glass to her lips and she drank. It was a delicious Sangria, at once sweet and tangy. He allowed her to finish the glass. The wine made her dizzy. A few drops spilled on her white dress, red as blood.

He grabbed her chin with his hand and forced her to look into his face, which he brought uncomfortably close to hers. He had a certain rakish attractiveness, with his shaven head, the gleaming earring and the goatee, but his eyes were hard and flat. The scar, a long thin white line against his tan skin, ran down his face like a snake.

"Anders tells me you're quite responsive to his training." He let go of her chin, but his eyes still moved over her possessively. "You've got the looks, no question about that." He narrowed his eyes and his voice went hard. "But beauty isn't enough. Not if we're to fetch the highest price."

He frowned, thick eyebrows knitting together. "I hope your time in solitary taught you a lesson, number thirty-eight. The word 'no' has no place in a slave's vocabulary. While Stephen was a little, uh, overzealous in bringing the point home, the sooner you learn to submit to your fate, the better off you'll be."

He stroked her cheek and she couldn't help it—she recoiled from his touch. He didn't notice, or, more likely, didn't care. He sat back, pursing his lips. "We have several potential buyers in the works. There's a man out of Texas, wants to buy a present for his wife. And another guy, very high up in the Kuwaiti government, Ibrahim Mahmud. He's bought from us before. But if you continue to be disobedient, I'll sell you to another man who has a reputation for sadism that makes Stephen look like a pussycat."

Julianna stared at him, her mouth falling open. He grinned, revealing large, square teeth beneath his thick mustache. "That's right, little girl. You better learn to play the game or pay the consequences." He reached for a shrimp and dipped it into a bowl of cocktail sauce.

He held it toward her. "Do you like shrimp?"

Julianna could barely focus on the question, her mind still reeling from his threats. "Come on, now, calm down. I'm not selling you tomorrow. You have time to redeem yourself. Meanwhile, answer the question. I like my slaves to have a good supper before we play, but if you'd rather not—"

"Yes, please, sir," she said quickly, reminding herself she had to eat when it was offered, never knowing when the next meal would come.

He nodded. "Good girl." He held the morsel to her lips and she opened her mouth, letting him feed her. The shrimp was delicious, fresh and tender, the tangy sauce the perfect complement. It occurred to her that food, which she'd always taken for granted in her previous life, seemed to taste better here on the island. It was as if her sense of taste and smell were heightened. Come to that, all her senses were heightened. She was always on constant alert, never at rest, never at ease, except maybe for a moment here or there in Anders' arms, between training sessions.

Jason fed her pieces of fresh mango and banana, interspersed with bread smeared with creamy cheese and more of the tasty shrimp. Julianna savored each mouthful, though she despised the man feeding her.

The sun was beginning to set, the ocean turning a deep blue-green, the wave caplets splashed with gold. Jason held a second glass of Sangria to Julianna's lips and she drank. She felt overfull and woozy and wished she could go lie down somewhere, even if just on the hard cot in a cell in the slave quarters.

No such luck. Jason set down the glass. "I trust you enjoyed your meal." He twirled one end of his mustache and smiled his wolf's smile. "Now it's time for dessert." She understood by his leer that he wasn't talking about food.

He led her into the back of the house, through the kitchen and living room along a short hallway to the bedroom. The room was dominated by a large bed covered in black silk, the ceiling mirrored above it. The headboard was of black wrought iron with chains and several pairs of cuffs hanging from it.

Jason led her to stand at the end of the bed. He unclipped her wrists. "Turn around and see what I've got for you." Reluctantly Julianna obeyed. Jason stood back, rubbing his hand over the crotch of his jeans, a leer on his face. Julianna looked away.

"Don't pull the shy act with me. Every woman wants a big hard cock and that's just what I've got. Hey! Look at me when I'm talking to you." Julianna forced herself to look at him. Though she kept her eyes on his face, she could see him unbuckling his belt in her peripheral vision.

"I generally prefer boys," he said conversationally. Julianna flashed to Pete and Jorge, and his comment about not needing their services that night. Jason continued, "With either sex I like a good fight, provided, of course, that I win." He guffawed as if he'd made a wonderful joke. Julianna wrapped her arms around her torso, not liking the direction of his remarks one little bit.

He pulled the belt from the loops of his pants and tossed it onto the bed. Reaching for the hem of his T-shirt, he pulled it over his head, revealing a very hairy chest and a stomach tending toward paunch, though he still looked powerful and strong.

She looked away as he removed his jeans and underwear, wondering what would happen if she tried to run from the room. The guards were gone—it was just Jason and her, but he was perhaps a foot taller and a hundred pounds heavier than she. She had her hands free, and she was probably quicker than he was. Could she get away? Did she stand a chance?

Before she could even ponder the merits or stupidity of this line of thought, Jason grabbed her roughly by the shoulders and threw her down onto the bed. He fell heavily on top of her. She could feel his erection hard against her thigh as his mouth sought hers. He forced his tongue between her lips.

Instinctively she pushed against him, twisting her head away, revulsion and fear rising inside her. He laughed. "That's right. Put up a fight, you sexy little whore." She squirmed beneath him and managed to twist out from under him, rolling to her side.

She swiveled upright but he caught at her shoulder, pulling her back down onto the bed. She was dizzy from the wine and from fear and couldn't seem to draw a proper breath of air. He loomed over her, his cold, dark eyes glittering. "Feisty girl. I like it." He put a hand on her throat and with the other slapped her cheek. She gasped, pulling with both hands at the hand on her throat.

After a moment he let her go, but only to grab the neckline of her dress, easily tearing the flimsy fabric and exposing her breasts. He bent over her, catching a nipple between his teeth. She cried out as he bit the tender nubbin. He sought the other nipple with his hand, twisting it hard between his fingers.

He wanted a fight? She'd give him a fight, the fucking bastard. She jerked her knee upward and felt it meet the soft flesh of his belly. He grunted and let go of her breasts. "Bitch," he swore softly but then he laughed. She rolled away again, managing to fling herself from the bed to the floor. She staggered to her feet, aiming for the bedroom door, with no plan other than to get out of the room, whatever the cost.

He rolled from the end of the bed, blocking her retreat. He hurtled toward the door, slamming it shut and turning the lock. She moved back, her eyes darting over the room, searching for another escape but there was none.

Still laughing, he lunged toward her, throwing her back down onto the bed. He fell upon her again, reaching for her wrists. While she struggled and twisted beneath him, he pulled her arms over her head and pressed his full weight on top of her. He pinned her to the bed and she could feel his cock pressing hard between her legs. She whimpered with fear.

"Please!" she gasped. "Don't do this!"

"I do what I want, little girl," he said. Using some of the hanging chain, he clipped her wrist cuffs to the headboard. He lifted himself from her to stand beside the bed. She lay panting, watching him as he reached for something on the floor. He faced her while he rolled a condom onto his long, thick cock.

"Ever been fucked in the ass, number thirty-eight?"

Julianna closed her eyes, pulling hard at the cuffs. He leaned over her, slapping her face again. "I asked you a question, cunt."

"No, sir," she whispered, her heart bouncing against her ribs.

He undid her cuffs and flipped her onto her stomach. He straddled her thighs and gripped a handful of her hair, jerking her head back. "That's good," he growled into her ear. "Been a while since I had a virgin."

She struggled beneath him while he grabbed her hands and clipped her wrists together behind her back. "You can stop fighting now. My cock is plenty hard. In fact, I suggest you just relax and enjoy it."

He leaned down over the side of the bed. She twisted back and saw he was holding a tube of lubricant. He squeezed the tube and smeared the clear gel over the head of his sheathed cock. Reaching for her hips, he pulled her to her knees and tossed away the torn remnants of the dress. "Press your forehead to the mattress for balance." She had no choice but to obey.

She felt his fingers hook beneath the elastic of the panties. "White lace for the little virgin," he said thickly. Savagely he tore them, ripping them from her body. "Yes," he oozed. "Oh, yes." She jumped as a finger moved its way over her asshole and pressed inside. Her body was trembling, her pulse leaping as she panted with fear.

He moved the finger slowly, pressing it in deep. "Relax," he said, his voice husky. "It only hurts if you tense up. Might as well take what's coming to you because I'm gonna give it to you good." A moment later, the finger was replaced with the gooey head of his cock. Julianna tensed and tried to move forward, away from the invading phallus, but Jason held her in place, his fingers digging into her hips.

The head pressed past the ring of muscle at her entrance and Julianna yelped in pain, panic moving through her. "Relax," he said again, his tone amused, which made what was happening all the more horrifying. "You're only making it worse for yourself. I'm not going to stop. You're gonna get fucked, so get used to the idea."

As the fat cock pressed inside her, Julianna felt as if she was being split in two. She knew it would hurt less if she stopped tensing her muscles, but she was too panicked and frightened to relax.

He held her hips, moving slowly but inexorably into her. After a while, despite her fear, somehow her body managed to adjust somewhat. It didn't hurt as much now that he was inside her. She could tolerate this. At least it would be over soon, she prayed.

"That's it, baby," he crooned. "I'm all the way in now." He began to thrust inside her, groaning while she did her best to vacate the premises, at least in her mind. She thought about the sea, the setting sun adding a layer of liquid gold over the blue. As droplets of the man's sweat fell over her back, she thought about Sandy, and freedom.

He grunted and rutted on top of her, pulling her toward him as he slammed into her, his balls flapping against her ass. Eventually he stiffened and, with a cry, jerked hard inside her and then fell heavily forward, crushing her flat as he collapsed on top of her.

She lay still beneath the deadweight, waiting for him to move, silently willing him to drop dead of a heart attack. No such luck. He rolled from her with a long satisfied sigh. She lay where she was, mentally taking stock of herself. She had survived the rape. It was better than a beating, or at least less painful. And the bed was soft and her tummy was full. She closed her eyes.

~*~

Julianna was pulled out of a light doze by Jason's voice. "Oh, okay. Send Jay and Vince then. I'm done with her." She turned her head to see Jason standing by the window of his bedroom, dressed again in jeans, though he remained shirtless. He was holding a small walkie-talkie like they all carried, staring out the window at the darkening sky. She realized he was calling for the guards to remove her back to her cell. Then she took in the full import of what he had just said. Jorge and Pete must be occupied elsewhere. Jay and Vince were coming. This was her chance to help Alma.

Jason slipped the walkie-talkie into his pocket and turned to look at her. "You're a hot piece of ass, you know that? Seems almost a shame to sell you."

Julianna didn't know what to say to this, and so said nothing. Was he insinuating she would take Alma's place, once Alma was sold? Had Alma once been as determined as she to escape? Had the years of enforced servitude and constant terror worn her down into compliance? Would the same thing happen to Julianna, to anyone?

She heard the sound of the ATV engine. Jason unclipped her cuffs and pulled her to her feet. He led her through the house, leaving the tattered dress and high heels behind. He took her to the front door of the house and opened it, pushing her out toward Jay and Vince, who stood waiting.

Vince did his usual, looking her up and down with his mouth hanging open, his face twisted into a leer. She ignored him, turning her head toward Jay as they walked her to the ATV. Knowing she might not get another chance, she whispered, "They've sold Alma. She's leaving the island in two weeks."

Jay jerked his head toward her, his startled expression making it clear he hadn't known this, and also that he cared. A slow, dark flush moved over his neck and cheeks. "You could—" she started, but he stopped her with a look and a glance at Vince.

"What're you blabbing about, number thirty-eight?" Vince said, as they settled her between them on the seat.

"Nothing, sir," she said in what she hoped was a meek voice. How stupid she'd almost been, suggesting Jay should rescue Alma, right in front of Vince. Jay had said nothing, yet something in his face told her he understood what she'd been about to say. Hope began to surge, even while she realized she had no real basis for it. Maybe he would rescue Alma. And maybe, just maybe, they'd come back for her as well.

Her heart sank as she really weighed this possibility, realizing it was slim to none. If Jay did steal the boat and get Alma out of there, he would be a wanted man. No way would he risk himself for Julianna, who was nothing to him. She felt the tingle behind her eyes that signified tears and blinked them away.

Focus on what you can control, she told herself. *Never give up.*

They led her into the slave quarters, past two cells occupied by girls chained to their cots. Lights were out already, but the men carried flashlights. Vince unlocked the barred door and stood back while Jay, his hand on Julianna's upper arm, escorted her into the cell.

She lay down docilely upon the cot, glad just to be left alone at last. She was relieved she'd been returned to the quarters instead of the solitary confinement hut. As Jay bent down to attach the chain to her collar, he murmured, "Thank you."

He was long gone when she finally recovered enough from the shock to whisper, "You're welcome."

Chapter 12

Julianna stood beside the girl she'd dubbed Veronica. The Texan sat before them, sprawled out on a large sofa in the room to which Julianna had first been brought for inspection and the photo shoot. Veronica and she were both dressed in black satin bustiers, their breasts pushed up high, the cleavage deep, demi-cups revealing their nipples. The stays of the bustier dug hard into Julianna's sides and cinched her waist so tightly she could barely breathe. Both women were wearing sheer, black thigh-high stockings with lace tops, their feet shod in black stiletto heels. Jason stood just behind them, his hand on the back of each girl's neck.

Alma had dressed them both while Jason stood by, making comments and leering. Julianna had been aching to ask Alma if she'd been able to connect with Jay, but Jason hadn't left them alone for a moment, giving them no chance to exchange even a whisper.

"You okay?" Julianna had managed to mouth to Alma in the mirror when Jason wasn't looking. Alma hadn't replied, except by a duck of her head, her eyes filling with tears. Julianna's heart ached for her, though she realized that tonight, she too was being offered up for sale. The thought was almost too surreal to comprehend.

"You two girls are gonna be competing tonight," Jason had informed them, as Alma applied makeup and did their hair. "Blake couldn't decide which of you he preferred, so we'll be putting you through your paces, and may the best girl win."

Blake was the Texas millionaire Jason had referenced before, the one who was buying a slave girl for his wife. The girls had been told Blake's wife was also dominant, and they were looking to add a new slave girl to the stable.

As if in costume himself, the man was wearing a large cowboy hat and black cowboy boots, the pointed toes capped with silver. He was tall and lanky with a big nose and prominent Adam's apple, which kept bobbing as he stared at the two women forced to stand in front of him. He was holding a glass of amber colored liquor over ice. He sipped at it as he raked their bodies with a hungry stare. Julianna hated him on sight, but then, she would have hated anyone who sat there.

"Hooo-wee!" he exclaimed. "These are some top notch fillies. Turn around, slow like. Let me see those sweet little butts."

Veronica and Julianna turned slowly. Julianna felt her face burning. No matter how many times she was put on display and paraded like a piece of meat, she couldn't seem to shake the humiliation and embarrassment. She felt the man's finger on her ass, touching the spot where Stephen had marked her. She jerked reflexively away from his touch. "Shit, what the hell, Jason?" the Texan demanded.

Jason shrugged. "Her own fault. Don't worry, it'll heal nice. She learned her lesson, so it won't happen again, will it, thirty-eight?"

"No, sir," Julianna forced herself to reply.

"How 'bout their cunts? Nice and tight?" the Texan asked.

"Like virgins," Jason affirmed. "You know I'd only offer you the best, Blake."

Blake rubbed his hands together. "I can't wait to see how they handle the fucking machine. I've seen it on the porn sites, but the real thing has to be so much hotter."

"I have it all set up for you, Blake. We'll record the whole thing too. It'll make a nice little demo film." He chuckled. "I'm looking forward to the demonstration myself." Julianna couldn't quite imagine what a fucking machine was, but she was pretty sure she wasn't going to like it.

"You!" The Texan pointed suddenly to Julianna. "Come here and sit on my lap, sugar. I want to check you out."

"Do as you're told." Jason gave Julianna a shove and she stumbled forward, nearly falling over the seated man. He reached out, grabbing her and pulling her onto his lap. Wrapping a strong arm around her, he pulled her back against his chest. He smelled of expensive cologne, too much of it. Julianna gasped as the man pushed her thighs apart and roughly fingered her pussy.

Though her head was bowed, Veronica was watching through her thick, dark lashes, a small, superior smile on her face. *It'll be your turn next,* Julianna thought, remembering the look of cold triumph on Veronica's face after she'd beaten Ashley.

"Yeah, nice and tight," the Texan crooned, while he tweaked one of her exposed nipples with his other hand.

He fondled her for a few moments and then abruptly pushed her from his lap to the floor.

"Kneel on your hands and knees. Any slave we own needs to get used to being used as furniture. The wife says it's good training in humility. Me, I just like a place to rest my feet." He laughed and leaned over, pulling her roughly into position. Sitting back, he put his heavy booted feet on her back. Julianna stayed in position, preferring this degrading pose to being manhandled.

He reached for Veronica next, pulling her down onto his lap, adding more weight to Julianna's back. Veronica giggled and cooed as he touched her. "Responsive lil' thing, ain't she?" Blake said with evident appreciation. Did Veronica actually *want* to be sold to this man?

"She's one of our best," Jason affirmed. "Better trained than the slave you're using as a footrest. That little redhead still has too much spit and vinegar, but nothing you and Melanie couldn't handle."

Blake chuckled. "Melanie likes 'em feisty. She's actually talked about getting an assistant, a kind of head slave girl. Someone who can dish it out as well as take it, if you follow me." He did something that made Veronica giggle again. "I like 'em wet and ready, like this delectable little morsel here."

His boots were hard and heavy against Julianna's back as he held the other girl on his lap. Julianna closed her eyes, attempting to drift away, but couldn't quite manage it. She gasped and jerked at the sudden, sharp pain of something poking sharply into her side. She realized it was Veronica's stiletto heel. Had she done it on purpose?

"Dang, this little slave girl has me stiffer than a honeymoon hard-on." The Texan's accent was so thick, Julianna found herself wondering if he was laying it on like that on purpose. "Let's get this show on the road so I can see how these two handle a little pressure." The heavy boots were removed from Julianna's back and Jason pulled her to her feet using the O-ring at the back of her collar as a handle.

Jason led them through a small door behind the bar that Julianna hadn't noticed on her other forced visits to the building. This room contained a large X-shaped cross with cuffs dangling from the four points of the X and a strange looking silver contraption that looked kind of like a stationary bicycle. It had a large steel wheel with a piston attached to it. At the end of the piston was a long, thick phallus made of a gel-like clear rubber. A thick leather sling hung from long chains nearby, and two additional chains hung from the ceiling in front of the sling, with leather cuffs already attached.

"That's a beauty," Blake said, eyeing what Julianna realized must be the fucking machine. Jason nodded, moving toward the contraption. He switched on a motor at the base of the wheel and it began to turn, pumping the piston with its huge rubber cock back and forth. He flicked the switch, increasing the speed of the piston with a whir of its motor, making the cock pump wildly in the air.

Julianna shrank back, terrified by the menacing contraption. She stole a glance at Veronica, but couldn't see her face. Veronica tossed her thick mane of perfect, shiny black hair. Her full, pretty breasts were thrust forward, her back arched. Veronica was actually smirking toward the video camera set up on a tripod at one end of the room.

"I do like to watch girls licking each other's pussies," the Texan said. "How 'bout we kill two birds with one stone? Put one of 'em in the sling and have the other one sit on her face. While the first one's gettin' fucked, she can eat out the other one. First girl to come wins!" He laughed and Jason joined in.

"Excellent idea. Who would you like to do what? You call the shots tonight."

Blake stared at both girls, his small, piggish eyes moving greedily over them. "I think I'd like to see that big ol' dick rammed up the redhead's snatch. She seems kind of uptight to me. Let's see if she can lick cunt like she means it."

Julianna thought of Sandy and her sweet, shuddering sighs when Julianna had been forced to lick her to orgasm. While she'd almost enjoyed the sensual power of being able to give Sandy that bit of pleasure amidst the terror of their daily lives, she had a horrible feeling licking Veronica would be quite a different experience.

Veronica was hostile, pitting herself against the other girls in a bid for survival. While Julianna understood the girl's motives, and appreciated the fear that drove her, she also had the awful feeling Veronica almost enjoyed it when she got the chance to get a leg up at the expense of another girl. Instead of standing together, fighting in subtle, secret ways for each other, as Sandy had done, as Alma had done, as Julianna herself had done, Veronica seemed only out for herself, ready, even eager, to sacrifice someone else to spare herself pain or make herself look better.

Julianna's thoughts shifted abruptly as she stared at the huge rubber cock attached to the end of the piston on the fucking machine. There was no way that thing would fit inside her, she thought fearfully, as the two men pushed and jerked her down to the ground. Jason lowered the leather sling to the floor behind her and forced Julianna to lie back on it. It wrapped around her waist like a wide, thick belt.

The two long chains dangled from the ceiling in front of her, cuffs at the ready. Jason lifted her legs one at a time and locked each ankle into a cuff. Moving toward the wall, he turned the wheel on the pulley mechanism attached to the chains. As the chains drew taut, the lower half of Julianna's body was hoisted into the air by her ankles. He raised the chain that held the leather sling, lifting her body higher, until only her head and the tops of her shoulders were touching the ground. Jason returned and knelt beside her, grabbing her wrists and cuffing them with Velcro straps behind her back. The position was awkward and she swayed in the chains, fully exposed and helpless.

"Jason, sir," she pleaded. "Don't let him hurt me." Oddly, she found herself wishing Anders was there. He wouldn't let any harm come to her. But he wasn't there. No one was there who could help her. She was all alone. Even Veronica was the enemy.

Jason grimaced down at her, his eyes glinting. "You'll take what you're given, thirty-eight, and like it."

Julianna tensed as the head of the soft rubber cock made contact with her spread pussy. It was cold and gooey with lubricant as it was eased into her. She jerked in her restraints as she heard the machine's engine whir to life. The phallus pushed into her slowly but inexorably. It was significantly larger than a real man's cock, but at least the soft rubber was yielding.

She couldn't help the small grunt as the shaft filled her. The engine pitch increased and so too did the tempo of the piston.

"Squat on her face, thirty-three. Stick out that pretty ass so the gentleman has a good view." Veronica straddled Julianna's face, her knees on the floor on either side of Julianna's head. She pressed her pussy lips against Julianna's mouth.

"Lick that cunt like you mean it, thirty-eight." Jason's voice suddenly close to her ear startled Julianna. "Make her come or I'll make you wish you had never been born."

I already wish that, Julianna thought miserably. Angrily she shook the thought away. They had taken her body and her freedom—they would *not* crush her spirit. Still, hoping to avoid whatever horrible punishment he no doubt had in mind, she began to lick and suck at Veronica's pussy, trying to find the hooded clit with her tongue. She didn't taste sweet like Sandy had, but Julianna forced herself to focus on the task of arousing the woman she'd been ordered to pleasure.

The huge cock filling her forced a grunt from her with each thrust. Veronica was moving over her, grinding her pussy against Julianna's mouth as the cock inside her moved in and out. The piston's speed was increased, the cock pushing deep, in and out, in and out, pulling a moan from her despite the terrifying circumstances.

She realized she was panting against Veronica's pussy, her body edging toward an orgasm she couldn't control and didn't want. Veronica moved spastically over her and Julianna held her tongue stiff, allowing the other woman to basically masturbate herself against it. She knew they wanted her to come, and they wanted her to make Veronica come. While she couldn't stop either thing from happening, neither did she urge her body, or Veronica, on in any way she could help. They were taking this from her—she would not give it. She would not cooperate with the enemy, even if her silent, ineffectual protest went unobserved.

Veronica began to cry out in breathy, sweet moans and Julianna heard her own unladylike grunts as the huge cock pummeled her toward orgasm. All at once the climax moved over her, gripping her with fierce intensity as she shuddered and groaned between Veronica's suffocating thighs.

"Boy howdy!" the Texan cried enthusiastically. "I do believe we got us a tie!"

The thrusting piston was finally turned off, the huge cock withdrawn from her gaping sex. Julianna sagged heavily against the sling, trying to breathe through Veronica's musk. Finally Veronica was pulled away from her, leaving her face smeared with the girl's juices and her own saliva. She lay passive and dizzy, wishing only to be left alone.

No such luck. The moment her ankles were released from their chains she was hauled to her feet. Veronica, she saw, had also been pulled upright. They stood again side by side, considerably more disheveled than they'd been, both with their hair tousled. One of Veronica's stockings had fallen to her ankle. Both Julianna's stockings had been torn by the cuffs, she saw.

Blake moved in front of them, his hat tipped down so Julianna couldn't see his eyes. He pushed the hat back and leaned in close. "I like these girls, Jason. I like 'em both. But this present is for my wife. She told me to find a girl who ain't afraid to use a whip, you follow me? I need a girl who can give as good as she got, if she's going to be Melanie's whip hand."

He stepped back, continuing to eye the two women. Jason appeared beside him, a riding crop in his hand. He turned to the Texan. "Here's an idea. We'll have us a little wrestling match. Both these girls are strong and fit. I do enjoy watching a cat fight, don't you? First girl to pin the other gets to use this," he held up the crop, "on the other girl. We'll put the unlucky loser on the cross and the winner can go at her. Sound like a plan?"

Julianna cast a horrified look at Veronica, but she was watching the men, her mouth pursed in a coquettish smile. She gave an expert toss of her beautiful hair and thrust her breasts forward. While Julianna found herself hating the girl, she couldn't help but admire her acting ability. It had to be an act, surely? She couldn't actually be enjoying what was happening to them.

"Sounds like a bee-yu-ti-ful plan," Blake drawled. "Let the games begin."

Jason released Julianna's cuffs and stepped back. Before Julianna realized what was happening, Veronica had leaped for her, grabbing her hair and jerking her downwards to her knees. Julianna cried out, pulling at the girl's hands with her own, tugging Veronica down as well. Veronica let go of her hair and backhanded Julianna hard across the face. Julianna fell back, stunned and furious. She kicked out, trying to keep Veronica from moving any closer to her. Veronica was fighting hard, her dark eyes blazing.

Julianna had imagined some kind of fake struggle between them as they wrestled around the floor. She hadn't expected the sudden, vicious attack. Veronica fell on top of her, pushing Julianna's head back so it knocked against the floor, the pain cracking through her skull. Julianna struggled beneath her, kicking her legs in an effort to push the girl from her. Veronica was several inches taller and had the advantage with her position from above. She began to slap Julianna in the face, over and over. Julianna tried to roll from beneath her and nearly succeeded, but Veronica was too strong for her.

The men were hooting and whistling, enjoying the show while Julianna panted and twisted beneath Veronica, trying desperately to get the upper hand. Veronica moved forward, pinning Julianna's arms to the ground with sharp knees. She slapped Julianna again, so hard it made her ears ring. Tears streamed from her eyes and rage seethed in her gut.

"I'd say we have us a pretty clear winner," the Texan said. Veronica looked up at him with a saccharin smile. In that moment, Julianna twisted sharply beneath her, throwing her off-balance so she landed with an ungraceful thud on the floor. Julianna rolled toward Veronica, grabbing a fistful of her thick, dark hair and yanking Veronica's head back. As the girl fell back with a cry, Julianna scrambled upright and straddled her, pinning her shoulders to the floor with her knees. She drew her hand back, fisting it, ready to strike, a red film of rage clouding her vision and her thoughts.

She could almost hear the crunch of cartilage and bone, but before her fist made contact, she was roughly hauled up and jerked to her feet. She was breathing hard, adrenaline pumping like liquid fire in her veins. She twisted and flailed, trying to get away from the men, her focus still on getting back at the woman lying at her feet.

The men were laughing as they held her. Veronica was cowering, covering her head with her hands. "You got you two little hellcats, Jason," she heard the Texan say. The men laughed some more.

All at once the fight went out of Julianna, and she slumped against Jason, who held her upper arms tight with his large, strong hands. This was all wrong. She was directing her rage at the poor, stupid girl lying on the floor instead these two vicious thugs who had reduced her to something almost less than human.

"I gotta say, I'm leanin' toward the brunette," the Texan drawled. "My wife likes her meat a little darker, if you get my drift." As he guffawed, Julianna was never so glad to be fair-skinned in her life. "Let's see how she does with a crop," he added.

The two men hauled Julianna to her feet and forced her over the X-shaped cross. She had lost her shoes during the scuffle but they didn't seem to notice or care. Her breasts were completely out of the demi-cups that had held them and both stockings had fallen to her ankles. As they pressed her up against the cross, Jason bent down and pulled off the stockings, leaving her barefoot. They secured her wrists and ankles to the wooden cross, wedging her head into the V of the top half of the X.

She could hear the clatter of Veronica's high heels behind her. "Go on, darlin'," the Texan drawled. "You make good on this and my wife has got herself a new toy. We treat our girls real good. You play your cards right, you'll have your own personal slave girl. I bet you'd like that, wouldn't you, honey?"

"Yes, sir," Veronica breathed, her saccharine sweet voice curdling Julianna's stomach.

The first stroke of the crop landed right on the still-healing wound Stephen had inflicted on Julianna's left ass cheek. Despite a self-made promise to be silent, Julianna screamed. She twisted back to see Jason taking hold of Veronica's wrist. "Watch it, thirty-three. That's my merchandise you got there."

The slapping rectangle of stinging leather was focused elsewhere, covering Julianna's back, ass and thighs until her skin was flaming and Julianna found herself whimpering and begging, "Stop! Please stop! Please!"

"Mistress," Veronica said sharply. "Call me Mistress."

Julianna pressed her lips together, hating Veronica fully as much as she hated Jason and the Texan. Veronica struck her again, raining blows over her back and thighs. "Say it!" Veronica began to smack her inner thighs and then struck her pussy, a sudden, vicious blow that made Julianna gasp with pain.

"Mistress," she cried, giving in. "Please stop, Mistress. Please."

Mercifully, the beating stopped. It had been as brutal and relentless as any she'd received on the island, save for Stephen's caning on the beach. She waited to feel her hands and ankles released, but nothing happened. She heard the murmuring of the men and the clatter of heels and boots over the stone floor and then the sound of a door shutting. When she could catch her breath, she managed to pull her head from the V of the cross. She twisted her head around to get a view of the empty room.

Were they just going to leave her here? In his eagerness to close the sale, had Jason forgotten about her? She waited, listening hard but she could hear nothing through the door. Her fingers felt cold and her skin burned from the thorough cropping. She was thirsty and achy and longing to be released, even if it was only to be led back to her cell.

After some minutes, she finally dared, "Hello? Is there someone there? Can I please be let down?" There was nothing but silence. She closed her eyes, willing the panic rising in her gut to still. Someone would notice she was missing, surely. When they did lights out, they would realize she was unaccounted for.

Was she glad Veronica had "won" and thus been sold to the peculiar Texan and his horrid wife? There was still the Kuwaiti man, waiting in the wings to add her to his harem. Would the Texan have been a better choice?

No. It was better like this. At least she would remain on the island a while longer, which meant she still had a chance to escape. She refused to admit she still had no idea how she could get away. She would not give up hope. She would remain vigilant and alert for the slightest opportunity.

Her ears perked sharply at the sound of a doorknob turning. She twisted her head again as it opened, her heart thumping, afraid Stephen had come to punish her for the Texan's choice.

Instead, she saw the handsome face of Anders poking around the door. "Julianna, my poor angel!" he cried, rushing toward her.

Julianna was stunned to realize she was glad to see him. Tears of gratitude pricked her eyes. She blinked them away.

Chapter 13

Though he cuffed her wrists behind her and attached a leash to her collar, when Anders led her from the building to the slave quarters, he kept his arm around her shoulders, pulling her close as they walked. He'd unhooked the uncomfortable and now completely askew and torn bustier, dropping it on the floor and giving it a little kick of disdain.

"Jason called for Jorge but I wanted to come get you myself." He ran his hand over her back and bottom, pursing his lips though he said nothing more. He looked model-handsome as always, his thick golden hair set off by a deep blue silk T-shirt that hugged his broad shoulders and strong, masculine chest.

Julianna wasn't used to being out this late. The night sky was studded with a million twinkling stars against the black velvet and the sound of the ocean was soothing as tiny waves lapped gently at the shore. It seemed as if they were the only two people on the island. For a moment she had a wild thought of elbowing Anders hard in the gut, then kneeing him with all her might in the groin. She would head out into the cold dark sea, taking her chances in a desperate bid for freedom. But, cuffed as she was, she knew she didn't stand a chance.

Anders pulled her closer as they walked, nuzzling the top of her head with his chin. He let her go only when they reached the side door of the quarters. She expected to be placed in one of the empty cells, but Anders led her instead to the training room he used for their daily sessions.

Putting a finger to his lips, he had her stop just inside the door of the room. Moving toward the far wall, he pressed a switch mounted there and then glanced up at the black globe in the ceiling where the camera and microphone were housed. Julianna followed his gaze and saw that the ubiquitous red light at its base was no longer glowing.

Anders removed Julianna's leash and wrist cuffs. He moved toward the bed and sat, pointing at the floor in front of him. "Kneel up as I've taught you." Very curious as to why he'd turned off the camera, Julianna knelt with her bottom resting on her heels, spreading her knees wide, lifting her chin and thrusting out her breasts. Her forearms rested, with palms facing upward, on her thighs. She looked straight ahead, focused on the blue silk of his shirt, willing her face into a neutral, vacant expression.

She could feel his eyes moving over her, lingering on her breasts. In spite of herself, she could feel her nipples hardening beneath his gaze. She could almost feel the bite of the clover clamps he sometimes used. Each time he clamped them, he would make her come, stroking her with a relentless, perfect touch with one hand, while tugging at the clamps to make them tighten with the other, blending and fusing the pleasure and the pain, not stopping until she'd come again, and again, and again…

He leaned forward and tucked a strand of her hair behind her ear, the gesture almost tender. She kept her eyes on his chest, waiting and wondering what was going on.

"Julianna," he said softly. "The connection between a trainer and his slave is a very intimate one, especially the type of sexual training I do. One has to be careful to keep one's feelings separate from the task at hand. It's one reason Stephen gives the girls numbers."

Julianna showed no reaction. He had asked no direct question, therefore she need do nothing but keep her position. She was a statue. She was made of stone.

"Julianna. Look at me. Look into my eyes." She obeyed, lifting her eyes to his face, to his piercing blue eyes beneath the straight blond brows. "When they took you away tonight for your audition with the client, I tried to tell myself it was a good thing. You were deemed ready enough to be offered for sale. I had done my job and that was that."

He took a breath. "I've trained many slave girls. This is the first time…" He trailed away. What the hell was he trying to say? Why couldn't he at least ask her up onto the bed to say it? Her knees were killing her and she was exhausted from the night's ordeal.

As if he'd read her mind, Anders patted the bed beside him. "Come here. I want you close to me." Julianna rose and sat beside him. He took one of her hands, holding it in both of his. "I know it's been hard for you, Julianna. To be taken from all that you know and forced into this strict training regimen. But you have blossomed under my careful hand, along with your other training here. You have learned that pleasure and pain, along with submission and obedience, go hand in hand.

"You were a spoiled young American girl with no sense of a woman's proper place, but in only a few weeks' time you have been remolded into a yielding, compliant and very sexual slave girl. I see how you respond to my touch—the quickening of your heart, the sweet blush on your cheeks, your cries of pleasure at the moment of ecstasy. I know you long to serve me, not as a numbered slave-in-training, but as *my* slave girl, my possession."

Julianna realized her mouth had fallen open. She pressed her lips together, trying to figure out what the man was saying. Did he really have the gall and complete lack of insight to imagine for one fraction of a second that she *liked* what was being done to her? That she was somehow complicit in all this? Had he really mistaken her physiological reactions to constant sexual stimulation as some kind of adoration, even love, for *him*?

Anders stroked her cheek, his touch gentle. In spite of herself, Julianna leaned slightly into the caress. "Tonight really brought home to me how easily I could lose you. The client didn't choose you, but that Kuwaiti gentleman might well snatch you up. I'm thinking of making a counteroffer for you. I'm thinking of taking you for my own; making you my personal slave girl. Perhaps, one day, if you merit it, you might even become my lover."

He regarded her intently, a small, superior smile playing over his lips, as if he'd just offered to make her his queen. Was he expecting her to kiss his feet, tears of gratitude spilling as she thanked him for the huge honor of becoming his personal fucking property?

She kept her face as impassive as Jorge and Pete did, but inside she was reeling. Too many thoughts and emotions were crowding her head. Would it be better to be owned by Anders, a known quantity, than some Arab sheik? She imagined this Mahmud guy as short, fat and old. Would she become part of a harem, imprisoned in a strange country on the other side of the world? Was the devil she knew better than the one she didn't?

"Before I make my decision," he went on, "I need to claim you completely. That's something I rarely do with the slaves-in-training. I reserve the benefit of my body for only the select few. Tonight I will make an exception for you, Julianna. I've chosen *you*."

A sudden nearly uncontrollable impulse to giggle welled up in Julianna. She suppressed it, aware Anders wouldn't take well to being laughed at. What a pompous, deluded asshole he was. Yet, he held her very life in his hands. The urge to laugh quickly died.

He stood, stripping off his shirt to reveal a smooth, tan chest with well-developed pecs, the nipples like flat brown coins above six-pack abs. He pulled down the zipper of his pants and slid them past muscular thighs. She couldn't help staring. Despite who and what he was, not to mention his absurd delusions of grandeur, she couldn't deny he was absolutely gorgeous. His cock, even only half erect, was long and thick.

"Like what you see?" His voice was full of self-congratulatory confidence. It drew her up short, reminding her that the man was out of his fucking mind. He wasn't some potential lover misguidedly trying to impress her, he was a stone cold bastard, a cruel and evil man who took part in abducting innocent women and destroying their lives for profit and whatever twisted sexual motives he had.

She didn't answer, but he didn't seem to notice. He took a condom from the small bowl on the side table near the bed. Tearing it open, he rolled the sheath over his now fully-erect shaft. His expression hungry, he fell onto her, pushing her down on the mattress.

"I know you've longed for this moment," he whispered huskily into her ear as he maneuvered himself between her legs. "What torture it has been for you, brought over and over to the edge of sensual pleasure at my hand, only to be denied my cock. Well, no more. No more, Julianna."

His body was heavy and hard over hers. He pushed his thigh between her legs, forcing them apart. He licked his fingers and reached for her, pressing one of them inside her. He pushed a second finger into her, quickly finding that sweet spot that made her moan, despite what was happening. After untold hours of intimate exploration of her body, the man knew precisely how to touch her to draw out her reactions, and now was no exception.

He brought her quickly to the edge of an orgasm with his fingers, but instead of letting her come, he pressed the thick head of his cock into her. "Yes," he urged, as her muscles clamped involuntarily around the girth filling her. He groaned as he eased into her. Her body reacted in spite of herself, drawing him in, gripping him tight. "Yes," he said again. "Give in to your deepest desires. Submit to your true Master." He dipped his head, his lips parting as they touched hers.

She twisted her head away, pressing her lips together. She had taken the whip, the cane, the forced sex and the pain, but somehow the intimate act of a kiss was more than she could bear.

Anders stilled inside her and lifted himself over her. "You resist my kiss?" His voice was soft but tinged with cold iron. He reached for her chin, forcing her to face him. She closed her eyes, her lips still pressed together.

"Open your eyes." Slowly, reluctantly, she obeyed. He was staring down at her. "You're overwhelmed with my gift, I understand. I know this is unexpected. Once you belong to me, you will learn to submit with complete grace. Stephen's harsh methods are effective in the short-term to tame and break down resistance, but you and I will have all the time in the world. You will learn what it is to truly serve a real Master, one who appreciates what you offer."

He leaned down again, his lips touching hers, his tongue pressing between them. This time she opened her mouth, letting his tongue dance over hers as he moved inside her. His kiss was intimate, the invasion slow and sensual. She could almost believe she lay in her lover's arms, but the leather of her collar pressing against her throat reminded her otherwise.

Anders put his hands beneath her hips, lifting her up into him as he swiveled and moved inside her. In spite of her anger and fear, her body responded to his skilled movements. He put his arms around her, groaning as he thrust inside her. She understood in that moment that for the first time on the island, she had a kind of power over someone else. He was, in his own warped, sick way, making love to her. If he bought her, would their relationship segue into something approximating lovers?

She experienced a sharp, bitter amusement to think that for a fleeting moment she'd imagined she had any power over anyone. Anders had no concept of love, unless you counted narcissistic self-love. He hadn't proposed to save her from this place, he wanted to buy her. This moment in his bed was a gift for which she was expected to be grateful. No doubt, if he did pay Jason to claim her for his own, she'd be kept in some basement dungeon, a slave hidden from the world, completely at his mercy. A shuddered eddied through her at the terrifying thought. Anders moaned in response, no doubt assuming she was reacting to his movements. He began to pant as he thrust inside her. He held her close as he spasmed against her. She could feel his heart beating and smell his sweat.

She hated him.

Finally he pulled out and fell on his side next to her, draping a strong leg over her hips, nuzzling his face at her neck. She lay still as death, wondering what happened next.

Eventually he opened his eyes and lifted himself on one elbow. He pulled the used condom from his spent cock and dropped the sticky thing on her stomach. Inserting the tip of his finger into it, he scooped up some cum. He lifted the finger to her lips. "Take my offering," he said, as if he were Christ incarnate conferring his sacrament. "With this, I'll know you are ready to become my permanent slave. I'll make a counteroffer to Mahmud. Jason will give you to me. I will insist." He smeared the gooey cum over her lips, pushing his finger between them.

It took every ounce of willpower not to bite down, to sever his finger to the bone, such was her roiling, impotent rage at the bizarre and bleak twist her life had taken. Her future, which should have been wide open with glorious possibility and potential, had shrunk to a choice between two Masters.

She licked the salty cum from his finger, feeling another piece of her life, of herself, of what made her a unique individual, slip away.

~*~

The door flew open. "There you are!" Stephen came charging into Ander's training room, Jorge and Pete just behind him. Julianna gave a small cry and pressed against Anders, who had his arms around her, spooning her from behind. After his bizarre proposal to make a bid for her, she'd expected him to lead her back to a cell for the night, but instead he'd kept her with him. He'd cuffed her wrists and ankles before falling asleep, but still it had been the most peaceful and restful night she'd spent on the heinous island, wrapped in a strong man's arms, held close in his warmth on the comfortable bed beneath clean, soft sheets.

Anders sat up now and shook back his hair from his face. His voice was calm as he addressed Stephen, who glowered at them. "It's all right, Stephen. I should have let you know I planned to keep her overnight, but it was late and I didn't want to disturb you." He bent down, releasing the cuffs from Julianna's ankles and sitting back against the pillows as he casually removed her wrists cuffs, seemingly unperturbed by Stephen's intrusion.

"This is totally against protocol," Stephen barked. "What the hell do you think you're doing?"

Anders swung his feet over the side of the bed and stood, completely unselfconscious in his nudity. Julianna saw both Pete and Jorge stealing glances at his firm, sexy body but their faces, as usual, registered no emotion. Anders reached for his neatly folded stack of clothing and pulled on his shorts before answering. "I've come to a decision, Stephen. I'm going to make an offer for this slave girl. I have decided it's time I had a girl of my own."

Stephen's dark eyebrows rose high on his forehead. "She's already sold, Anders. To that Arab guy."

"No." Anders shook his head. "He has made an expression of interest only. I intend to talk to Jason this morning about a counteroffer."

Stephen shook his head, his expression one of disbelief. "Why the hell would you want to fork over that kind of money when you have all the pussy you want on this island? She's just a dumb cunt. A piece of ass. I don't believe she's submissive at all. She needs at least another month of serious, focused training to whip the devil out of her. That's what I told Jason, but he just wants to move the goods."

Anders frowned at Stephen, who grimaced back at him. Julianna could see there was no love lost between the two of them. "At any rate," Stephen said, squaring his shoulders. "As of this moment, number thirty-eight remains island property, and you've committed an infraction by keeping her overnight instead of locking her up. As head trainer, I'll be reporting this to Jason. Meanwhile, I can't punish you, but I *can* punish her."

Stephen moved toward the bed and reached out, yanking Julianna to the floor. She cried out and twisted toward Anders, expecting him to intercede, but he only stood there, hands on his hips, glaring at Stephen. At a gesture from Stephen toward the guards, Pete and Jorge moved in, hauling Julianna to her feet.

"Get number thirty-eight cleaned up and groomed for me. Then put her in the cage." Julianna was pulled from the room. As the guards hustled her along to the showers, she realized she had been expecting Anders to do something, say something, anything, to keep her from Stephen's clutches, but he'd done nothing.

Julianna was forced to pee standing up while the guards watched her. Then she was showered and shaved. While Jorge was drying her, Pete had his back to her, arranging something on the counter. He was wearing a tank top that showed quite a bit of his upper back. Julianna stared, noticing a series of red and purple stripes over his shoulders and upper back.

She tried to reconcile her now certainty that these two men were not free men, with how much freedom they were given on the island. They seemed to roam as they pleased. They were given whips, canes and keys to cells, huts and machinery. They were both tall and strong. Why did they submit to this treatment? What kept them here, when they had the strength and wherewithal to escape?

She realized she was to have no breakfast—she'd been asleep in Anders' arms when the guards had brought around the food cart. The men replaced her collar and led her to Stephen's torture chamber. She had expected them to place her in the tall narrow cage where she'd been forced to watch Sandy jerk the two of them off, but instead they led her to a corner of the room. Pete lifted a black sheet from what looked like a dog's crate, complete with metal bars and a small door. He crouched beside it and pulled the metal bar, allowing the door to swing open.

"Get in," he said. It looked too small for a person to fit. Surely they didn't expect her to get in there.

"I can't—"

"Get in," Jorge echoed. He pressed her shoulder hard until she buckled beneath his hand, falling to a crouch beside Pete. She looked at each of them beseechingly, but saw no yielding in their faces. With a sigh, she turned around, backing herself in an awkward crawl into the tiny space. By curling tightly on her side, she was able to lie down, her ass pressed against the back bars of the cage, her head touching the bars of the door as they closed and locked it.

The black sheet was draped over the cage and she heard the sound of the door closing softly. Alone, in the dark, Julianna felt hot tears well behind her eyes, but none fell. *Maybe*, she thought, *I have none left. I'm empty.* She thought of the words to a song she once knew. She couldn't hear the tune or remember the name of the band, but the words played in her head like a dirge. She felt *cold as a razorblade, tight as a tourniquet, dry as a funeral drum…*

Chapter 14

Julianna's eyes flew open as the blanket was pulled from the cage. She could see sandal-clad feet she recognized as Stephen's. He crouched by the cage and pulled back the bar that held the door closed. "Get out and kneel on the floor, ass in the air."

At first Julianna couldn't move. She must have been in there at least an hour and her limbs were cramped and folded. Stephen reached into the cage and caught hold of the O-ring at her throat, tugging her forward. As the blood flow began to return, her limbs were flooded with an unpleasant, painful tingling sensation. When he'd dragged her out onto the floor, he said again, "Kneel with your ass in the air, thirty-eight. Move!"

She struggled to get into position, glad at least she didn't have to stand. He moved behind her and struck her hard across her right cheek with his open palm. Not expecting the blow, she fell out of position, sprawling forward.

"Up! Up!" he shouted. "Give me that ass, you slut! You are a dirty, nasty little whore. I hope that Arab does buy you. I hear he gives his harem girls clitorectomies. You know what that is, thirty-eight? He's going to cut out your dirty little clit, so you won't go whoring around, trying to seduce your trainer. I don't know what you did to bewitch Anders, but I can assure you, it won't work with me, you whore."

He struck her again, even harder than the first time. She fell flat to the floor. He continued hitting her—hard, stinging blows that took her breath away. His words rattled in her brain, filling her with terror. She lay still, trying to absorb the pain, letting it flow through her, praying he would stop soon. He did, but only to yank her upright, hauling her roughly to her feet.

"What do you have to say for yourself, whore?" He pushed her against the wall and slapped her face. "Answer me!"

"I—I—," she gasped. "I didn't do anything wrong!"

He slapped her again. "You were found out of your cell. Reason enough for punishment."

The unfairness of his reasoning would have stunned her, if she hadn't stopped trying to reconcile anything that happened on this island. He didn't need a reason to punish her. It was that simple. He did it because he was a bully and a bastard. He did it because he could. Perhaps on some weird level he was jealous of Anders because Anders gave the slave girls what he could not. Or maybe he had a tiny dick and used all his dildos and torture devices as a twisted substitute for his own inadequacies.

Hatred flared like a hot white flame in Julianna's heart as Stephen forced her to the bondage table and secured the leather straps that held her down. She had done nothing wrong!

"I'd like to cane you until you bleed, but since your sale is imminent, Jason won't permit it." *Thank god for small favors, you prick,* she thought, but his words reminded her with a terrible finality of what was in store for her. She was to be sold to a man who would perform genital mutilation! The thought was beyond terrifying. The prospect of belonging to Anders no longer seemed quite as bleak. Silently she prayed he would be able to counter Mahmud's offer.

"The nice thing about electroshock," Stephen said, "is that it leaves no marks." He turned to his counter of evil toys and held up a thin dildo with wires attached. "You've been exposed enough to this now to take a little more juice. After all, this is a punishment." He laughed cruelly and Julianna felt herself trembling. "I think an anal probing should do nicely, coupled with this for your filthy little cunt." He held up a second, thicker dildo. His voice had grown calmer, assuming the clinical, dry tone he used when readying for a long, painful torture session. Julianna's blood ran cold and, despite the fact she was lying down, a wave of nauseating dizziness assailed her.

When he'd penetrated both her orifices with the phallic weapons, he turned the dials on the little black box in his hand, not stopping until her screams filled the room. Her body became an arc of rigid pain. When he finally released her from the current, she lay utterly spent, drenched in sweat, her mind as empty and dark as the inside of a coffin.

~*~

A crack of thunder jolted Julianna from a restless sleep. It was followed by a flash of lightening that lit up the cell for a moment, even through the small, high window. Another peel of thunder followed seconds later. She could hear the sound of heavy rain pummeling the roof of the building.

There was a sudden booming sound, like something exploding, making Julianna jump. She strained to hear what was happening outside. After a few minutes she heard the sound of voices and muffled footsteps outside the building. She sat up, hugging herself, her ears pricked, her heart beating fast. What was happening?

After the extended torture session with Stephen, she'd been taken back to her cell and left alone until the evening meal. Anders hadn't called for her or come to her. She had missed his comforting touch, even if it was coupled with what he termed erotic suffering. Why hadn't he called for her? Was he in trouble too, as Stephen had hinted? Would he even be permitted to make his counteroffer?

When Jorge had placed her food on the floor, she thought he looked especially subdued, though she realized she was probably projecting her own feelings onto him. Suddenly it had occurred to her, based on snatches of conversations and bits of evidence she had pieced together, what might be troubling him. Alma had once been owned by Jason, and it appeared Jorge and Pete were still his property. Could it be that Jorge was sad Alma had been sold and was leaving the island?

Taking a gamble, Julianna had said gently, "You're going to miss Alma, aren't you? I'm going to miss her too. She was kind to me." Jorge glanced sharply at her, but per his usual, had said nothing.

Another crack of thunder shook Julianna from her recollection. She could hear someone shouting and she listened hard, trying to decipher the words over the rushing sound of the rain. She made out the word *generator* and then *fire*. Fire! Anxiously she looked around her cell. The building itself was of wood and concrete. Could it catch fire? What would happen to her and the other women held prisoner in its cells? Anxiously she tugged on the chain that was locked onto her collar. She felt behind her, fingering the padlock that kept the hated leather always around her neck. She stood and moved toward the bars of the cell, gripping them as she looked out into the dark of the hallway.

She startled as she heard the sound of one of the side doors being opened. Someone was coming for them! Yes, of course they were. They wouldn't leave such prime "property" to be burned up, surely not. She should have known better. She waited, expecting the hallway to be flooded with light, but it remained dark, save for a small thin beam, the beam of a flashlight.

The light stopped in front of her cell, and she could make out the tall, broad shape of a man. He held the flashlight just below his chin and she saw it was Jorge. "What're you—" she began, but he hushed her with a warning finger to his lips.

He unlocked her door, moving quietly, though she sensed a kind of tense urgency in his actions. What the hell was going on? Again he put his fingers to his lips. Reaching for the key around his neck, he unlocked the chain attached to Julianna's collar. Then, to her amazement, he unlocked the padlock that held the thick collar in place at her throat and unbuckled the hated thing, letting it fall to the floor.

She touched her neck with the fingers of both hands as she watched him remove a small backpack from his back and withdraw from it a rain poncho, a T-shirt and a pair of cotton pants with a drawstring waist. He held them out. "Put these on. Hurry!" Bewildered but happy at the chance to be somewhat clothed, Julianna did as he said.

"Where are we—"

"Alma's waiting for you. Hurry."

Leaving the cell door ajar, Jorge pulled her along, gliding quickly but silently along the hallway. Instead of his usual clomping boots, Julianna saw that his feet were bare. He opened the door cautiously and peered out. Blinding flashes of light illuminated long silver needles of rain that punctured the dark. Julianna saw Pete then. He was pressed against the side of the building. He gave Jorge a nod. "You're clear. I'll wait a few minutes and then I'll sound the alarm that one of the girls is missing. It'll go just like Jay planned. They're still all over at the generator hut so you have a few extra minutes. Go!"

Julianna heard the sound of men shouting and realized the whole island was dark. Recalling the boom, she realized the generators that provided electricity to the island must have been hit by lightning. Jorge took her hand, pulling her along a path toward the palm trees, which were swaying wildly in the wind.

Alma's waiting for you… Just like Jay planned. Pete had watched them go, clearly in cahoots with whatever was going on. Julianna knew Alma had been sold, but she wasn't due to be removed from the island for a few more days. What did Jay have to do with what was going on now? Could it be he was waiting with Alma on the boat? Waiting for Julianna?

Jorge was trotting now, moving with sure feet through a maze of trees, Julianna barely able to keep up with him. She was drenched despite the poncho, and would have fallen behind, but Jorge kept tight hold of her hand, spiriting her along through the slippery grass.

Escape! *He's helping me to escape, though god knows why or how!* It was the only explanation that made sense. As this realization clicked into place, it sent an immediate jolt of adrenaline through her veins. It felt like a flooding river inside her, powerful enough to take anything in its path. She sprinted along beside him now, her heart thumping in her chest, water streaming over her face.

They came out on the shore, near the dock where the boat that had brought her to this dreaded place was kept. The engine was running and she could make out two silhouetted forms in the boat. "Hurry!" Jorge urged.

Julianna saw it was indeed Alma in the boat, along with Jay! A bubble of wild, tumultuous joy rose inside her, but she refused to let it burst. She'd been through too much over the past weeks to trust that all was as it seemed. This could still be some kind of horrible trap. She turned to Jorge. Breathlessly she demanded, "What about you? You and Pete? Don't you want to get away?"

Jorge shrank back, shaking his head. "No."

"Julianna!" Alma called softly, her voice nearly lost in the wind and blinding rain. "Hurry. We waited for you. Hurry!"

Jorge let go of her hand and Julianna ran toward the small dock. Jay reached out for her, swinging her in and onto the seat beside Alma. Julianna saw Jorge disappear back into the trees as Jay eased the boat slowly out into the rocky, turbulent waters.

Julianna looked back toward the island. She could see the fire now, a small orange and yellow conflagration through the trees. The boat was listing sharply as Jay executed a turn. It occurred to Julianna they were probably risking their lives, going out like this in such a storm, but she didn't care. Better to die like this than be sold and mutilated, her spirit crushed, her body in chains.

She turned back toward the open sea with one word beating like a drum in her head. *Free. Free. Free!*

~*~

Tendrils of dawn light worked their way through the morning mist. Julianna waited huddled on a bench outside the American Embassy in Bridgetown. She clutched her purse, inside of which her passport waited to prove her status as an American citizen.

It had taken about an hour to make what Jay told them was normally a twenty-minute trip to Barbados from the island. Though the heavy rain had stopped shortly after they'd left the dock, the seas remained choppy and Jay had given both the women lifejackets to wear beneath their ponchos. He was wearing one as well. While Jay concentrated on piloting the small boat, Alma and Julianna huddled close together. Alma had whispered in Julianna's ear, telling her they had her to thank for her escape.

"Jay might not have found out, if it weren't for you, dear Julianna. They knew he was fond of me." She ducked her head, smiling shyly as she said this. "They didn't want him causing a stir so they had planned to send him away until I was sold. He pretended to go along, not even telling Vince he knew the truth. He was just biding his time until he could rescue me. He had told me to be ready—that he would come for me one night. Jorge agreed to be our messenger. I didn't expect him to make the journey during this weather, but he said this was the best time—when they least expected it."

She paused and then smiled, the rain pouring down her face like tears. "He loves me. No one has ever loved me before, Julianna. Except maybe my mother, but she died when I was four. Jay's leaving the life. He's got savings. We're going to disappear. He promises they'll never find us."

Julianna didn't voice her misgivings about how reliable a man like Jay might be. At least he'd taken

Alma away from the nightmare on the island, and her imminent sale. Perhaps love made redemption possible, even for someone like Jay.

Alma had produced Julianna's purse from the floor of the boat. It was so strange to see it. It was like it belonged to another world, another life. "We'll leave you in Barbados," Alma had said. "Go directly to the American Embassy. Don't go to the local authorities. Some of them are in Jason's pay. They might send you back to him."

Julianna assured Alma she would go straight to the embassy. "I can't believe you all took such a risk for me. I'm so grateful. But what about Jorge? Won't he get into trouble for letting me out? Why didn't he want to come with us?"

"Jay took care of the whole thing. He had all the same keys Jorge and Pete have. He told them to blame him for what happened. It's very unlike Jorge to do what he did. I doubt he'll even be suspected."

"Why did he do it?"

"For me. He did it for me. Remember, I too used to belong to Jason, though only for a year or so. There was one time..." Alma frowned and bit her lower lip, the memory clearly troubling her. "You may know from your own experience, Jason likes to play rough. Especially with the boys. He wants them to fight back, but not *too* much. One time he was really tearing into Pete and Jorge just couldn't take it anymore. He dared to get in the way. He told Jason to stop. He threatened Jason, something you just don't do. I wasn't there—I heard afterwards from Pete. Jorge wouldn't talk about it. But Jason turned his rage on Jorge. He let Pete go, but he strung Jorge up between two trees and caned him until he bled. He left him strung up all night and into the next day." She had leaned closer as she told the story, glancing nervously from left to right as if, even on the high seas, miles from the island, she might be overheard. "When Jason was away from the house, I snuck out back and gave Jorge water, a whole canteen's worth. He drank every drop. Pete gave him a banana. We didn't dare do more, for fear of being discovered, but Jorge never forgot it."

Julianna thought about her time in the solitary hut, and how Jorge had given her water from his canteen, and Pete had offered her the bruised banana. One good deed planting the seed for another…

She had asked Alma then, "Why didn't he come with us! Get away from the island and that horrible man! There's room for Pete, too."

Sadly, Alma shook her head. "They know no other life, Julianna. Jason picked them up from the streets when they were boys, Jorge from Mexico City, Pete from Philadelphia. They've been his personal slaves all this time. I begged Jorge to come, but he only shook his head. I know it's hard for someone like you, someone who grew up free and strong, with family around you, to even imagine, but Jorge and Pete have been living this life for so long, it's all they know. It's their comfort zone. They feel safe in their chains, if you can possibly grasp that concept."

"The other girls!" Julianna said suddenly. In her own wild relief and joy, she'd forgotten about Rachel, Ashley and whoever else remained imprisoned on the island. "What about them? We can't leave them there."

"We couldn't risk it. Even getting you—Jay was against it but he did it for me."

Julianna nodded. For some reason Alma seemed to love this man—this man who had taken part in the abduction of who knew how many women. And, it seemed, he loved her as well, at least as far as such a person was capable of loving someone else. Maybe Alma would be his saving grace—that which made him human again.

When they had docked safely in Barbados, Julianna had turned suddenly to Jay, who hadn't said a word during the tense and difficult journey through the storm. "Please," she said. "Tell me how to get back there. I've got to help the other girls. We have to shut down this whole horrible operation."

Jay had backed away at first, shaking his head. "We'll be gone, Jay," Alma had entreated. "Maybe Julianna's right and the authorities will be able to shut the whole thing down. Stephen and Jason will have a hard time tracking you down if they're stuck in jail."

Jay had smiled then, apparently enjoying that particular visual. "You have a piece of paper and a pen in there?" He pointed toward her purse. Julianna pulled out a pen and rummaged for the index cards she'd packed to write her impressions of her spa vacation for the nonexistent advertising company that was supposedly footing the bill. Jay wrote a set of numbers with N and W beside them and handed it back to her. "Those are the longitude and latitude coordinates of the island. It's uncharted, but using those, they can find it."

With that, and a quick hug from Alma, Jay had hailed a cab and put Julianna into it. By the time she'd asked the cabbie to take her to the American Embassy in Bridgeport and then turned around to look through the back window, Alma and Jay had disappeared.

Julianna watched now as a young woman in a navy blue business suit approached the front door of the embassy and unlocked it. As she pulled the door open, Julianna stood and approached her. The woman stepped back, looking mildly alarmed, and Julianna realized she must present quite a picture, her hair tangled and matted from the storm and the winds, dressed in this old rain poncho and baggy pants.

She dug into her purse, quickly pulling out the small blue-jacketed passport. "My name is Julianna Beckett. I'm an American citizen, and I need help."

The woman's eyes widened. "You're Julianna Beckett? Of New York?"

Julianna's pulse quickened. "You've heard of me?"

"Yes. You were reported missing over a week ago when you failed to return to your job after your vacation. The embassy checked with the spa and they had no record of you ever arriving. I have the bulletin in the office. Come inside, please, and I'll take your statement. Do you have next of kin I can call for you?

Are you hurt? Were you harmed in any way? Where have you been?"

Julianna's eyes filled with tears which spilled over onto her cheeks. It was finally sinking in for real. She was free! She wouldn't be sold to an Arab sheik or a sociopathic slave trainer. She would no longer be kept chained, beaten and tortured daily, fed barely enough to stay alive. She was free! But she wouldn't forget the other girls, at least the ones left on the island, the ones not yet beyond help or hope. She wouldn't rest until they too were free, and the men who had abducted them were behind bars.

She held out the index card she'd been holding for hours in her hand, checking it from time to time to make sure she'd memorized the coordinates correctly. "Here. This is where I've been."

Epilogue

Julianna sat on a bench in the small park near her apartment building, the novel in her hand unopened. A small dog came running out of the copse of trees along the edge of the park, a red rubber ball in its mouth. Skittering past her, the dog stopped in front of a tall young man in faded jeans and a black T-shirt. Julianna couldn't see his face, but something about him seemed familiar.

Hopefully he wasn't another damn reporter, hanging out where she lived to spy on her. The story had been picked up before she even made it back from Barbados, and splashed all over the newspapers upon her return. Because Anders was so good looking, his photo had been prominently featured in the headlines, his intense blue eyes with those lashes tipped with gold, staring soulfully at the camera as though *he* were the victim in all this.

During the first few weeks back, reporters had dogged her every move. One guy, who kept telling her to call him Jimbo, actually had the gall to say, "Come on, Julianna, you can be candid with me. Off the record, wasn't it kind of hot? At least on some level? You know, being kept naked and chained, serving that movie star-handsome guy Anders, being 'forced'—" he had actually used his fingers to indicate quotation marks around the word, "—to serve his every sexual whim?"

It had taken all her self-control not to punch the asshole in the jaw or better yet, knee him in the groin. Instead, she'd snapped, "No, it wasn't *sexy* to be repeatedly tortured and raped. I wonder how you'd like it if someone shoved an electric rod up your penis and turned it on. I mean, as long as the woman doing it to you was sexy. Would that be *hot* for you, Jimbo?"

Armed with the longitude and latitude coordinates Julianna had provided, the authorities were able to locate the tiny island, and had swarmed the place, rescuing the remaining women and arresting the men. Julianna had tried to find out what happened to Jorge and Pete, if they were also being tried as criminals, but she hadn't been successful in learning much about their fate. She had told the FBI agents about their situation, but the agents were all so deadpan and difficult to read that she had no idea if they even believed her. She tried, too, without success, to learn what had happened to Jay and Alma. Jay, as part of the slave ring, was a wanted man. She could only hope he was doing right by Alma, and that they managed to create a new and happier life wherever they ended up.

The little dog ran past again, wagging its tail like a windmill as it hurtled toward the tossed ball that had landed not too far from Julianna's feet. There was a time she would have bent down to retrieve the ball and toss it for the eager puppy, but now she just sat there, watching.

She'd done little in the nearly two months since her return, other than spend hours in the halls of the Federal

Building, or in the office of the therapist assigned to help her process what she'd been through. She slept until nearly noon each day, seeing no point in getting up. She hadn't returned to her job at Sophie's Salon. She hadn't done much of anything. It was as if she'd been frozen in time, her life stopped dead in its tracks by the abduction.

It was hard to fathom sometimes—that what had ended up being less than three weeks in captivity should have ripped her life so thoroughly to shreds. She no longer knew who she was or what she wanted anymore. When she looked into the mirror, she sometimes didn't recognize herself. There was a haunted look in her eyes that belied everyone's assurances that everything would be okay. Would things ever be okay again?

This time the dog ran right up to her, dropping the ball and panting, its little pink tongue lolling as it gazed up at her with liquid golden-brown eyes. The ball forgotten, the dog began to sniff the toe of her shoe. The man appeared and scooped the dog into his arms, laughing. "Sorry, she's still a puppy. Very short attention span."

He had curly, light brown hair in need of a cut, kind brown eyes and a nose slightly too big for his face. Suddenly Julianna placed where she knew this guy. They'd met at a party. At the time she'd found him attractive, but she was just coming off a not-so-serious relationship with another guy who had turned out to be a total jerk, and she wasn't eager to leap back into the fray just yet. She'd had a little too much to drink, as she recalled, and they'd talked and flirted some, but nothing had come of it.

He was looking at her too, tilting his head. "I know you," he said, smiling. "We met at Caitlyn Johansson's birthday party back in January. Do you remember? I'm Jake. Jake Goldman and this is Gracie, my new puppy. You're Julianna, right? Julianna Beckett?"

She nodded, waiting for him to add something about seeing her haggard face in the newspaper under the headline: *Queens Girl Held Captive on Slave Island* and dreading the inevitable follow-up with lots of intrusive questions about the experience, but he didn't say a word. Was it possible he didn't know about it? Was he the only person in New York who didn't?

Gracie gave a small yelp and leaped out of Jake's arms onto the bench beside Julianna. The puppy gently rooted her little wet nose against Julianna's jean-clad thigh. Julianna couldn't resist stroking the impossibly soft floppy ears.

"I'm sorry," Jake said. "She thinks just because she's so cute that everybody automatically adores her."

"It's okay," Julianna found herself saying. "I like her." The dog had rested her head on Julianna's lap and closed her eyes with utter puppy trust. Julianna found her heart, which had felt frozen, beginning to thaw a bit.

Jake's smile broadened into a slightly lopsided grin, his eyes twinkling. "She likes you, too. Is it okay if I sit?"

Julianna nodded. For the first time in a long time she actually felt a small tug inside, a whisper of desire. Ever since her escape, she'd been so shut down, shut off from everything and everyone around her. Was it possible she was finally ready to rejoin the human race?

Jake sat beside her, the puppy a buffer between them. Jake patted the dog's head. His hand was large, the fingers square and blunt tipped with short, clean nails. Julianna had a sudden urge to put her hand over his, but she did not. Instead she asked, "What kind of dog is she?"

"Gracie's a mutt, but with a healthy dose of cocker spaniel," Jake said. "I have no business having a dog, since I'm in my third year of medical school, but she was just so sweet, I couldn't resist." He stroked the dog's head with obvious affection. "This guy in my class was taking her to the pound, can you imagine?"

"How come?"

"He lives in an apartment building. No dogs allowed. He'd found her abandoned near the building, but his super found out soon enough what he was up to and that was that. I'm lucky. I rent a small house near here with a decent-size backyard, so Gracie can hang out while I'm at the hospital." Julianna remembered now, Jake had told her at the party he lived in Queens too, not far from her building on Harmon Street. He leaned down, lightly kissing the top of the puppy's soft head. Gracie awoke and lifted her little face toward him, licking the tip of his nose.

Julianna wanted to say something to keep the conversation going, but her mind was oddly blank. Since she'd been back, she'd found it hard to engage in the small talk and easy banter that had been second nature before the abduction. She realized Jake was watching her, a sad smile on his face.

"I read about what happened to you. I'm sure the papers just gave the bare bones about it all and probably got half of it wrong, but from what I read, you've been through hell and back. I'm so sorry for what you must have gone through."

Julianna looked away. She didn't want to talk about this with a near-stranger. It was hard enough talking about it with her therapist. But instead of diving in with personal and humiliating questions, as others had, he said, "I have to say, I really admire you, Julianna. If it wasn't for you, those other women on the island might never have been freed, and those monsters would still be out there trafficking in human cargo. You're a hero. That must feel pretty good."

Julianna stared at him and a small warm feeling moved through her at his words. She had been described repeatedly in the news as a victim. There had been token mention of her part in busting the setup, but the focus had been more on what she'd suffered while on the island. It sold more papers, apparently.

"I never thought of myself as a hero," she said slowly, but found herself smiling. The smile fell away as she thought about the ones who hadn't made it. "There was a girl there. I called her Sandy in my head. *She* was a real hero." Julianna pressed her lips together before more words could tumble out. She knew if she started talking about Sandy, who had apparently disappeared into the vast ocean without a trace, she would start crying, and that was the last thing she wanted to do.

"I'm sorry," she said. "I'm not really good company right now." She shifted on the bench, angling away from Jake so he wouldn't see the tears in her eyes.

"Hey, I understand. You came to the park for a nice peaceful chance to get some reading done," he glanced at the unopened novel in her hand, "and we just came barreling over. I'll tell you what. There's a nice outdoor restaurant near here, Sadie's Café. It's just two blocks up on Fairfield Avenue." He pointed that direction, adding, "They're cheap, and dog-friendly."

He stood, scooping the little dog into his arms and setting her down on the grass. "Gracie and I are heading over there for some iced coffee and some of the best chocolate pound cake in the city. We'll probably be there a while—I have the whole day off and no plans other than to enjoy this spring sunshine. So if you change your mind..." He smiled and shrugged. "And if not today, well, Gracie and I come to this park whenever we can, now that the weather's nice. So maybe we'll see you around."

Julianna nodded. "Thanks," she managed, wondering if she'd simply lost the ability to connect to another human being, or if it was something she could retrieve, over time.

Jake stepped around the bench, reaching for and pocketing the little red rubber ball while Gracie yipped excitedly by his feet. He attached a leash to her collar and turned back to Julianna, smiling. "Don't be a stranger, okay?"

Julianna nodded and Jake began to walk away, the little dog pulling him along in a frenzy of puppy enthusiasm. Without looking back Jake called, "Sadie's Café. Fairfield Avenue. Best chocolate pound cake this side of the planet."

She found herself grinning, something she thought she'd forgotten how to do. She watched them leave the park, her mind whirling. Jake had been so nice, so easygoing. He was good looking too, without being too pretty-boy-handsome as Anders had been. More importantly, though he knew of her ordeal, she hadn't felt that wave of pity and horrified curiosity most people seemed to approach her with.

What would it be like, to talk to someone about what had happened who didn't leap to analyze or judge or recoil in horror and disgust? Someone who would just listen? She sensed Jake would be a good listener.

Suddenly a memory came to her, sharp and clear, of the first night she'd spent in the slave quarters. She'd been terrified, the full impact of her situation really hitting home as she lay, chained and collared in the tiny cell. She had told herself then that she wouldn't let her life end before it had really begun. She had promised herself she would find a way to escape, and that once she was free, she would live her life as if each day were her last.

Yet she'd spent the last two months wallowing in self-pity, nearly paralyzed with depression and lingering fear. Where was the celebration—the joy? She had done it! She *had* escaped and she was *free*! She was young and strong, with her whole future still ahead of her.

She looked around her, noticing for the first time a cluster of bright yellow daffodils that seemed to have sprung up overnight. She stood, tucking the novel under her arm to be read another day. With a smile, she headed down Stanhope toward Fairview. Iced coffee and chocolate pound cake? Why not?

Available at Romance Unbound Publishing

(http://romanceunbound.com)

A Lover's Call
A Princely Gift
Accidental Slave
Alternative Treatment
Binding Discoveries
Blind Faith
Cast a Lover's Spell
Caught: Punished by Her Boss
Claiming Kelsey
Closely Held Secrets
Club de Sade
Confessions of a Submissive
Continuum of Desire
Dare to Dominate
Dream Master
Face of Submission
Finding Chandler
Forced Submission
Frog
Golden Angel
Golden Boy
Heart of Submission
Heart Thief
Island of Temptation
Jewel Thief
Julie's Submission

Lara's Submission
Masked Submission
Obsession: Girl Abducted
Odd Man Out
Perfect Cover
Pleasure Planet
Princess
Safe in Her Arms
Sarah's Awakening
Seduction of Colette
Slave Academy
Slave Castle
Slave Gamble
Slave Girl
Slave Island
Slave Jade
Sold into Slavery
Sub for Hire
Submission Times Two
Switch
Texas Surrender
The Auction
The Compound
The Cowboy Poet
The Master
The Solitary Knights of Pelham Bay
The Story of Owen
The Toy
Tough Boy
Tracy in Chains
True Kin Vampire Tales:

Sacred Circle
Outcast
Sacred Blood
True Submission
Two Loves for Alex
Two Masters for Alexis
Wicked Hearts

Connect with Claire

Website: http://clairethompson.net
Romance Unbound Publishing:
http://romanceunbound.com
Twitter: http://twitter.com/CThompsonAuthor
Facebook:
http://www.facebook.com/ClaireThompsonauthor